Margaret Anne Curtois

The Romance of a Country

A masque. Vol. 1

Margaret Anne Curtois

The Romance of a Country
A masque. Vol. 1

ISBN/EAN: 9783337345013

Printed in Europe, USA, Canada, Australia, Japan

Cover: Foto ©Andreas Hilbeck / pixelio.de

More available books at **www.hansebooks.com**

The Romance
of a Country

A Masque

BY

M. A. CURTOIS

AUTHOR OF 'JENNY,' 'TRACKED,' 'MY BEST PUPIL,' ETC.

Laszt uns auch so ein Schauspiel geben !
Greift nur hinein ins volle Menschenleben !

They seek a country.

VOLUME I.

LONDON
T. FISHER UNWIN
PATERNOSTER SQUARE
1893

CONTENTS

---o---

THE COUNTRY IS SOUGHT

THE COUNTRY IS SOUGHT

The Romance of a Country.

———o———

AN old tradition tells us that there was once a land known as the Fair Country—an *old* tradition, dim with the dust of centuries, but retaining some traces of beauty, like other echoes of far-off, golden times. History is silent, for one thing at least is certain, the Fair Country is no longer numbered with the nations.

If we question the legend further, we learn that this Land Beautiful lay in the midst of mountains, a sunny, fertile spot. Some glimpses we gain of blue hills and pleasant pastures ; some of its people, indolent and passionate ; a few of the wealth of its rulers, and the splendour of their palaces. Its poets sang—'The Spirits of the Sunbeams love our land ; they warm it, and dance on it, and prefer it to any other country. For there is no such beautiful land on the surface of the world !'

A

If this were all, if there were no more to be said, we might be content to leave the Fair Country to the peace of the nation which has no history. But it is impossible to deny that in the midst of these memories we become conscious of unexpected echoes, stormy as the muttering of distant thunder, or the crashing of a war-chariot over grass and flowers. Historians might deduce the conclusion that even the voices of tradition cannot contradict what we know of human nature. The tradition, however, is in this case so fragmentary that it is difficult to compare it with serious history.

It is not, then, my intention to concern myself with anything of more weight than a story, a romance gathered from the legends of a country, which may possibly serve for the amusement of idle moments beneath summer leaves or beside the winter's fire. Unhappily, such a legend, dealing principally with individuals, belongs almost of necessity to evil times ; for such times, whilst they ravage a country, by way of compensation display individual characters in bold relief, writing their history in signs as lurid as fiery letters upon a shrivelled page. Do we call those happy who possess no such distinction ?   Alas ! even obscurity is not always possible.

With these few words let us attempt to unite and from such fragments of this ancient romance as we possess, always remembering that we tread

on doubtful ground, that no certain geography or
history can be expected, and that such names and
phrases as have come down to us are not more
than echoes of long-forgotten words. Accepting
such echoes for lack of better guidance, let us ask
what they tell us of the Fair Country.

They tell us, first—for some sentences of explanation are needful before the commencement of
our romance—that the mountains in the midst of
which our country was situated were themselves
the home of many warlike tribes ; and that these
wild races, as plunderers and robbers, continually
threatened the existence of the Fair Country
(Alidrah). Amongst these mountain tribes there
was one more powerful than the others, with
which the history of the Alidrah became miserably
linked ; but of this race we shall hear so much in
future that for the moment it is unnecessary to do
more than mention it. A few words will set forth
the unfortunate occasion which connected it with
the affairs of the Fair Country.

It appears that, some generations before our
romance begins, there was a revolution in the
Alidrah, whose people revolted against the govern-
ment of the Nobles, who had been for ages Priests
and Rulers of the land. A sudden tumult over-
turned the work of centuries ; and the unfortunate
Estria *(Noblemen)*, in danger of their lives, fled,
with but few exceptions, from the country, and

sought such shelter as the mountains could afford.
The people of the Alidrah, meanwhile, soon re-
penting of their conduct—which had been only
influenced by temporary causes—restored the remaining Estria to power, and prepared a decree
which should recall the Exiles. It was almost
completed when, like a sudden earthquake, unexpected tidings convulsed the Alidrah, destroyed
irrevocably the prospects of the Exiles, and convinced the most doubtful of the justice of their
banishment. It is necessary to give some attention to a circumstance on which our tale depends,
as from a central thread.

We have seen that among the wild races which
surrounded the Fair Country there was one more
powerful, more dreaded than the rest; one, it may
be added, which gathered to itself every feeling of
horror with which the rest were feared. According to the statements of the Alidrah, the people of
this tribe were a mis-shapen race, with swarthy
faces, and dark glowing eyes, lit by the fiends from
whom they were descended. Their name, Rema,
could be translated *Dwarf;* and with the horror of
superstitious dread the Alidrah declared that the
ancestors of its enemies were Ero-a (malignant
gnomes, who work in mines). With the most
bitter enmity, with national abhorrence, with all
the intensity of religious hatred, the Fair Country
resisted the cruel adversaries from whose depreda-

tions it had often suffered. And when it became known that the Exiles, in despair, had fled to the *Fiends* (for by that name they were called), their countrymen, in a frenzy, declared their wealth confiscated, and themselves for ever banished from their native land. This national decree relieved the fury of the people, and the Alidrah was again restored to peace.

Years passed. The Fair Country continued undisturbed, secure under the rule of the remaining Estria; while the Exiles, surrounded on every side by enemies, lingered out wretched lives upon the mountains. One by one they died, and their miserable descendants became scattered for the most part, and sought homes in distant lands; only a few still remaining as a tribe, and defending themselves against their wild neighbours as they could. A worn-out remnant, unprotected, powerless, it seemed evident that the Fair Country need not fear them. And, indeed, under ordinary circumstances it would have had no cause for fear, but there arose a danger which was not ordinary.

It is with this danger and its consequences that our romance will be principally concerned. Its peril was personal, twofold; already through these mists of ages there loom two figures, distinct though shadowy.

Some introduction is necessary here, though at

that time the figures seemed almost mythical. The
first, and at first most dreaded, was Ursan, leader of
the Rema ; the other, the young chief of the exiled
Estria.   An old—a young leader ; a menacing
conjunction, which excited to the utmost the
alarm of the Alidrah.   And the terror of the
nation found adequate expression in the wild
traditions which gathered round their names.

These traditions (to accept for the present those
which were most reasonable) called Ursan, the
king and leader, an old man—supreme over the
Rema, who were devoted to him ; a monster of
iniquity, but none the less beloved ; a man of
genius, given to vast schemes of conquest which
he kept in his own breast and revealed to none ;
a cruel master, a perfidious truce-breaker, soft as
a leopard, but with the fierceness of a wolf.   In
such terms, accompanied by the wildest stories,
was the Maravel of the Rema described by the
Alidrah.   Meanwhile, concerning Alvo the Exile
there had been many differing rumours, uniting
at last in a terror like the oppression of a dream.

That horror had been reached by degrees. The
first accounts had represented the chief of the
Estria only as a sickly youth, beautiful in face,
but otherwise contemptible, and still retaining the
marks of some years of slavery.   There was a
story that he had summoned all the Exiles, and
entreated them to assist him in the recovery of

their land; and that this appeal had been heard with the utmost scorn, and only responded to by ninety men. Loudly laughed the Fair Country, though the time was not far distant when Alvo and his ninety were not held to be a jest. For, from the moment when it appeared that Ursan favoured the young leader, the young leader loomed as a cloud, dimly seen, but dangerous.

Already he had become the subject of the most extravagant rumours, when, like the thrust of a real knife through dreams, there appeared in the Alidrah the swarthy faces of men who called themselves messengers from Alvo. These men belonged to the race of Kroni *(apes),* and could not speak the language of the Alidrah; presumably they were held of little value, or they would not have been risked on an errand so dangerous. The message, however, which was read in the Great Hall *(Estrifad)* was in the language of the Alidrah and eloquently expressed, although it was impossible not to be sensible that it had the tone of a master rather than that of a suppliant. It demanded for Alvo and his ninety Nobles the restoration of the lands which their fathers had possessed, promising that as soon as this restitution was accomplished the Exiles would be faithful to the interests of the Alidrah. The name of Ursan did not appear in it; but, according to custom, there was tied to the scroll a ring, and on this was engraved the ominous inscription, '*Alvo, Son-in-War of the Maravel of the Rema.*' It may be imagined with what return of frenzy the Fair Country received the name of its enemy.

For the moment that frenzy prevailed. The Kroni were assaulted by the mob, and only saved that they might carry back the answer—a reply without salutation, expressed in these few words:

'Let Ursan and beardless Alvo do their worst!'

With this message, perchance more resolute than dignified, the ambassadors vanished like an ugly dream. An interval followed, during which the wildest fancies began once more to spread through the Fair Country.

Naturally, these broken, feverish rumours attached themselves now to the name and history of Alvo; for it was obvious that the young leader, once despised, had become a danger which the land had cause to dread. It was whispered that he drank blood, that demons guarded him from wounds, that his beauty had the power of magic, that his mother was a gnome—and still, the more greedily these tales were devoured, the more legends rose to feed the terror of the land. 'Let Alvo come!' cried the wise. 'If he delays much longer there will not be a man who will dare to fight with him!' The desperate wish was granted; for not many weeks had passed before it was evident that Alvo came.

News was received that Ursan, at the head of a host of Rema, was marching over the western side of the Ekelfah *(Northern Plain)* ; whilst Alvo, with his ninety nobles, and a horde of mountain warriors, advanced as a separate danger from the east. The Estria had done their best to prepare for an invasion, and had summoned the Nira *(Border Tribes)* to their assistance ; but the various tribes of the Nira, disheartened, terrified, appeared to waver, and would not send back a reply. The armies of the Alidrah were scarcely organised when suddenly other messengers appeared ; and with the terror which their embassage inspired there mingled a deep sensation of relief. This time there was no danger for the ambassadors—Nira, taken captive by the old Maravel.

The message was rude, abrupt. It declared, without salutation, that the Fair Country might tremble, for Ursan was approaching ; and that, when he entered it, their insolence should be punished, and they need not hope for mercy. Even now, however, he was willing to allow them a short truce, during which they might decide in what manner to receive him ; and his brother-leader, Alvo, his friend and son-in-war, united with himself in this kindness, although it was unmerited. Attached to this message was a copper ring, on which were scratched the two names, ' *Ursan— Alvo.*'

So there was a truce, an invaluable pause, during which it was possible to make some preparation ; yet the Fair Country trembled, and the Nira hesitated, and the pause seemed only the stillness before the storm. It is during this truce, this pause before the storm, whilst the Alidrah trembles, and the Nira hesitate, and Ursan and Alvo are indulging each in his own dream of ambition, and the breezes of early summer are scattering the spring blossoms—it is at this time that we will enter the Fair Country.

THE WEDDING-NIGHT OF
ESTRI ASCAR.

It is possible for the slightest circumstances to have an abiding influence on the destiny of nations ; for which reason the wise lay hold on trivialities, and turn them, as they turn other events, to serve their will. In the book of trifles any word may be important—a sudden skirmish, a quarrel or dispute, the little differences that lead to alienation, the chains of a captive, the lights of a wedding-night. A nation's destiny has been known to waver on threads that seemed even of less size and weight than these. For no link of a chain has any separate value ; its value lies in its connection with the rest.

I.

O Youth, rose-crowned, yet full of strife,
　Craving uncomprehended joys,
Hearing the desperate fight of life
　But as a far-off, pleasant noise !

IT is the wedding-night of Estri Ascar.   And who
is Estri Ascar?

Roll back, mists of ages, and show a young
nobleman of the Fair Country.

I see a great hall lit with the glare of flaming
torches, and hear the wild music of many instruments, and am conscious of the voices and movements of a great crowd of guests gathered round
the banquet, or standing in the hall.   And there,
in the midst, in a carved, jewelled seat, I see a
young man clad in dark green, with white roses on
his head, strong in limbs, dark, dark-eyed, with a
face burned by the sun—a face full of life and fire,
and the eagerness of youth, on which time has
engraved no difficult lessons yet.

13

This is Estri Ascar, now holding his bridal feast, the lord of a gaunt rock at the north of the Alidrah, the descendant of the only distinguished nobleman who was left in the land when the principal nobles fled. Upon this Escola, or Guardian Rock, the first attack of the Rema must break, almost certainly; for whilst to the south of it lay the blossoms of the Alidrah, the desolate northern plain stretched to its base. But neither this circumstance, nor the fury of the country, nor the predictions of sages, nor the wrath of the Estria, nor the certainty that he would be immediately called away to join the army, had deterred Estri Ascar from holding his wedding feast. And there were those who declared that the torches of this wedding-night were giving light to an action that would set fire to the land.

It might have been that terror which was reflected strangely in the eyes of one from whom terror would not have been expected—the maiden who was seated, adorned with regal splendour, at the side of the young nobleman—Estri Ascar's bride. A fair bride! whose beauty was framed by shining hair, crowned with white flowers, enfolded in gold-embroidered robes, in itself justifying the position she occupied as the centre of observation, the princess of the feast. And yet her eyes, deep blue-grey, and wide open, looked into the distance, as in bewilderment; and in spite of the stiffness of her golden robe it could be seen that her childish form was quivering. No stranger, beholding her for the first time, could have escaped the impression, that, in spite of her magnificent attire, she was but the captive of Estri Ascar's bow and spear, compelled by the force of his will to hold a false state at his side. On the dark glowing features of the bridegroom, nevertheless, was only the expression of gratified desire, so complete that he did not even turn his face towards the maiden who shared his bridal state. Life crowned Estri Ascar that night; he had gained the prize he wanted, in spite of furious, determined opposition; and though terrors were looming over his country and himself, he was prepared to meet them cheerfully. Let the enemy come! let them attack the Escola! let himself be summoned to the army and the conflict! let anything, everything, break on him at once, if only he were permitted this one night with his bride! So dreamed Estri Ascar; and it would appear that the bride he had chosen was also vision-haunted. Meanwhile, with furtive expressions that dared not tell all they thought, the wedding-guests glanced at the bridegroom and the bride. They had all been summoned to *hold the wedding-night* —the marriage-festival of the Alidrah.

And now—music! For although all through the feast the unseen musicians had never ceased to

play, it was not till this moment that they filled
the hall with the favourite Bridal Chorus of the
land. It rushed like the wind—and then a sudden
pause made preparation for the voices of the singers.
They rose, clear, piercing, in the ancient Bridal
Song, for ages familiar to the Alidrah.

> Come to the marriage-feast ! Over the mountain's side
>   Spirits are hasting the tidings to tell.
> Come to the marriage-feast ! Down by the river's side,
>   Starlit, they joyfully dance in the dell.
>   Here in the marriage-hall,
>   Here may no trouble fall,
> Here every heart may be blithesome and gay.
>   Come to the bridal here ;
>   Sorrow and lonely fear
> Pass at the sound of our music away.

The song was interrupted by the surging throbs
of music ; and then again, still more wild and sweet,
the voices rose—wild, mournful, since even in the
Bridal Chorus the note of unmixed joy could not
be sustained. The sudden change did not strike
as a surprise on those to whom it had been long
familiar ; it was the consciousness of real danger
that passed like a shudder through the company.

>   Here burn the torches bright,
>   Here rings the music light,
> Garlands are wreathing the Bridal Hall here ;
>   Far be the halls of woe,
>   Lonely and dim below,
> Where flows the Stream of Ill, darksome and drear.

There, past the Spirit-Sea,
There may no bridal be—
Death strikes so soon at all, greatest and least—
There, in the Shadowland,
Bridegroom nor bride may stand ;
Oh ! while you yet have life, come to the feast !

Into the inner Hall broke the wail of the unseen
singers, but the music answered by a triumphant
crash. It was time, for the pulses of every guest
were quivering : at this strange bridal all things
seemed ominous. And now at each pause another
sound was heard, the noise of the rising wind
which shook the curtains. At every interval of
the rushing Bridal Chorus the cries of its gathering
storm were audible.

What did he think?—the young man of unusual
aspect who sat behind Ascar as the bridegroom's
friend, the mark for glances which, even in the
bridegroom's presence, revealed suppressed hatred
almost openly. Young as the Estri, but absolutely
different, pale, dull-haired, with lithe figure and
keen eyes, he sat bent forward, with his glance on
the company, as one long used to sustain the scorn
of men. What links, ominous even in this ill-
omened wedding, connected this guest with the
bridegroom and the bride ; and what were the
circumstances of real or imagined danger which
added this wedding-night to the perils of the
nation? Let us pause for an instant in the midst
of the festivities to gather for ourselves such ex-

planation as we can.   Whilst the rude bridal music
sweeps round Ascar's hall, let us ask how such
music became possible.

The Estri was an orphan.   The visions of the
past, which could not but be with him on this
eventful night, could show him little besides the
grey rock of the Escola, where, with but one short
interval, he had lived all his life.   A gaunt rock,
looking over the barren, restless plain, as if it were
always expecting enemies—as drear a spot, and as
desolate in appearance, as could have been found
in the whole of the Fair Country!   Here Ascar
had lived, detained by the last wish of his father,
who had dreaded for his son the luxuries of the
Alidrah, and had therefore commanded that until
the boy reached manhood he should remain with
his servants upon the Guardian Rock.   It was a
lonely life, but the dark-eyed boy had been happy
in learning every day to climb and ride, in listening
to stories of his ancestors, and imagining projects
for a splendid future.   Ignorant, inexperienced,
full of passionate prejudices, he was yet strong,
healthful, with limbs full of energy, unlike the
father who had died of luxuries, or the wan mother
who had known how to read the stars.   The name
she had chosen for her only son loomed indeed
with an ominous meaning, *Evil Star;* but its
influence had not been powerful enough to rob the

hope from Ascar's heart, or the strong life from his limbs. And whilst the proud noblemen of the Fair Country despised him as a barbarian, little better than a savage, the Estri, alone in his gaunt solitude, was developing the most vigorous impulses. These were recognised when, through the fears of the Fair Country, there spread strange rumours of Estri Ascar's friend and bride ; and in wrath and amazement the people cried out loudly that the barbarian Estri would set fire to the land. It is necessary for us to seek some explanation of the terror which haunted Ascar's wedding-night. We have seen the bridegroom's friend seated near the bridegroom—it is to his story that we will listen first.

The magician's son, Olbri ! With eyes watchful, keen and pale, Olbri sat behind Ascar at the wedding-feast, his lips possessed by an expression of disdain which appeared to include both occasion and company. Amongst those who cast stolen glances at the Estri's strange acquaintance there was not one who could fathom his expression ; but all resented its habitual look of scorn, and would have expressed that resentment if they dared. And, meanwhile, though conscious of their familiar enmity, Olbri sat listening to the wind and wedding-music—in each vibration, either of storm or instruments, hearing mingled sounds of remembrance and foreboding. To the wizard's son this occasion of Ascar's bridal brought no sensations of festivity, but he would keep by the side of Ascar whilst he could—it might be the last service he would render him.

Olbri thought of his Escola cavern. In the days of Ascar's father, he had lived there with his own father, the magician Olloto—so called by his neighbours, for the old man himself disclaimed all magic, even the study of the stars. In vain! he was a student with scrolls and instruments, and learning was not tolerated in the Alidrah. It was evident that he was in league with Evil Spirits, and that the Great Spirit required a sacrifice. Olbri could remember how, in a twilight before dawn, he had rushed to find help when his father's cavern was attacked, returning with some acquaintances to find his home ransacked and desolate, but in time to save his father, who was being led out to be drowned. The infirm old man, bruised and terrified, never held up his head after that experience, or left his cavern-home again.

Other memories! The son of the sorcerer could still recall the time when he watched day and night by the side of his father's couch, until forced, by the command of that father, to go out into the world that in some distant land he might find a home for both. He remembered also how one

evening at the time of sunset, whilst he was
wandering amongst the Nira, a pale, quick-
witted boy, sudden terror seized him, so that,
on that same night, guided only by the stars, he
began to hasten home. And then, though this
memory he dared not recall, he knew how, in a
morning twilight, he had lingered outside the
cavern, listening to silence with a beating heart,
until he had entered to find his father's body on
the ground. In that instant he had thrown himself upon the corpse in the passionate hope that
one death would seize them both. It had not
done so, but from that time his pale, keen eyes
wore the look of one who has been terrified.

Certainly it had never been his fancy in those
days that he would be a guest at the wedding-
feast of the Lord of the Escola—those solitary
days during which the mercy of his neighbours
only reached to the fact that they left him to
himself. He was the son of the sorcerer, in touch
with Evil Spirits, doubtless, some day, to be banished from the land—but he was still young, and
because he was so young they left him for a while
to develop in solitude. Olbri lived in his cavern,
a bold, skilful hunter, buying food with the skins
of the animals he killed ; bitter, solitary, his one
passionate affection reserved for the spot where he
had laid his father's corpse. Yet, with the incon-
sistency of an untrained nature, he would often

spend many days without looking on the grave,
and then, flinging himself upon it, lie there for
days and nights until almost too feeble to crawl
in search of food. Strange memories to mingle
with Ascar's wedding-music! But they made part
of life itself to the son of the sorcerer, although he
turned, shrinking from the pain they caused, to
the thought of the friend who had been kind to
him. If the Nira slave had come between Ascar
and himself it was not less true that Ascar had
been generous.

Their acquaintance had begun strangely. On
a summer evening, as Olbri with his hands full of
flowers was climbing down the Escola, he was met
by some of Ascar's servants with a message from
their lord, abruptly forbidding him to climb there
again. Only on that morning the son of the
sorcerer had been summoned before a council in
the town, severely questioned with regard to his
lonely life, and informed that if he were accused
of evil he would be banished. The decree
was a threat of dishonour to his father, as
well as separation from his father's grave; and,
being still possessed by the consciousness of
danger, Olbri made no reply to the servants of the
Estri. But he was not the less enraged, and all
that night he lay on the floor of his cavern in
a conflict, divided between his own wish for
defiance, and his dread of dishonouring his father's

name. The struggle ended in a foolish com-
promise ; he climbed up the rock in the grey
morning before dawn ; and the servants of Ascar,
ready for an early hunt, looking down into a chasm,
saw him gathering crimson flowers. They had
long dreaded the son of the sorcerer, and now he
seemed given into their hands, an easy prey ; they
laid wait for him, seized him, and with ungentle
handling conveyed him at once into the presence
of their lord. Olbri made no resistance ; and with
the first rays of the sun he found himself standing
in the court of the Escola.

A distinct remembrance on Ascar's wedding-
night ! The courtyard lying in the golden light
of dawn, and its owner in the midst of it, a dark-
eyed lad, twisting in confusion the handle of his
hunting-knife. On every side rose the voices of
his servants—the offender should be scourged,
should be driven from the land, should lose his
ears ; the young offender listening meanwhile
without a word, although his face became hot and
cold by turns. All at once he shook himself free,
and striding boldly up to Ascar—whom every
instant had made more miserable—he struck him
with the back of his hand across the face, crying,

'That is a challenge, Estri, if thou hast the
blood for it ! '

Ascar had the spirit ; he flung away his knife,
and the two lads became locked in desperate

conflict. The servants did not interfere; it is possible that they were anxious to see of what stuff their lord was made.

The rest can be soon told. The son of the sorcerer had known harder days than those of the nobleman; and, slender as he was, had the unbending sinews of one whose life has been spent in self-defence. Ascar was flung with violence to the ground; and, at once conscious that victory has its dangers, Olbri rushed to the side of the courtyard, which lay on a natural platform, and cast himself down upon the rock below. The fall was greater than he had anticipated; he was bruised and stunned, unable to raise himself; in a few more moments, once more in the servants' hands, he was carried again into the courtyard of the Escola. Ascar had risen, and with renewed perplexity stood looking down on his victorious antagonist. He lay there, pale, bruised, breathing heavily with pain, this boy of his own age who had fought with him!

The spirit of an Estri spoke.

'The Escola does not turn away the wounded. Take him into the hall, and do all that is needful for him.'

Unwilling looks were exchanged amongst Ascar's servants, but they did not venture to disobey their master; though they lifted their captive from the ground with so much roughness that the sudden

pain forced a low cry from his lips. Ascar turned
round, indignant, and with youthful impulsiveness
seized on the first object with which he could
make amends; he snatched from the ground the
scattered crimson flowers, and piled them in a
cluster on the bruised breast of the boy. Even as
he did so, Olbri caught his hand, and clasped it,
and kissed it, weeping passionately. From that
moment—the moment when their hands touched
—the son of the nobleman knew the son of the
sorcerer.

What need of more words? The lads grew up
together, though Olbri continued to live in his
cavern as before; they rode, and hunted, and
studied side by side, and were so often seen with
each other as to appear inseparable. And yet the
position of each remained unchanged; Ascar,
dark, strong, handsome, was the descendant of
noblemen; whilst Olbri, pale, lithe, keen-witted,
was still the wizard's son, who would some day
commit an offence for which he would be banished
from the land.

'I will stay in my father's country,' Olbri cried
out once to Ascar, in one of his rare moments of
passion; 'it shall never be said that my father's
son was banished; I will stay in his land and win
honour for his name.'

Ascar pitied and praised, though his own inexperience hindered him from complete comprehen-

sion of his friend, the quick-witted friend who taught and laughed at him, and on whom in return he bestowed a nobleman's protection. It need not be added that one result of that protection was that the wizard's son was more hated than before; but Olbri had been so long used to enmity that it is possible he scarcely realised his danger. Dark glances had always followed him, although none so dark as those which pursued him furtively at Ascar's wedding-feast. And yet he was not to blame for a ceremony which he had neither occasioned nor desired.

No. Ascar had been alone on that fateful autumn evening when, as he paused to draw rein by the side of a brook, there rose from the long grass a maiden, roughly clad, but with shining hair which fell down below her knees. Slender, lovely, with the expression of one awakened from a dream, with deep eyes that seemed seeking some country far away, this was evidently one of the Water Akbare *(good spirits)*, who had appeared to him that he might worship her. It was only when she became conscious of the young man's glance, and colour mounted into her frightened face, that he realised this could not be a spirit, this must be only a woman after all. This must be Ered, the lovely Nira slave . . . he had heard of her . . . Ah! she was beautiful!

Late, late that evening, through a purple glow of

sunset, did Ascar linger by the side of the Nira slave, leaning against his horse whilst he looked at her, and she stood before him, trembling, obedient. He had scarcely spoken to a woman in his life; Ered had scarcely spoken to a man ; they met together as if from different worlds they had suddenly found and recognised each other. Answering his questions with a slave's obedience, she told of her attendance upon a widowed Estra—herself a captive taken by the Estra's husband from the tents of the Nira after these had lost a battle. And then, yielding to the spell of sympathy, she spoke of a severe mistress, of a lonely life, of passionate longings for her unknown kindred, of vows to devote herself to the gods of her unknown country. To the Estri, accustomed to the sceptical son of the wizard, this beautiful vision with spiritual eyes seemed to be a being in communion with spirits, touching chords in his nature which had not before been stirred. Late, late they lingered ; and when at last they parted she remained in his fancy with clasped hands and drooping head ; whilst Ered, distressed as one overwhelmed with guilt, lay down in the long grass and concealed her face. She had never felt more in need of her Akbare, and yet, perchance, never so far away from them. In the long grasses, against which her face was crushed, her faint utterances of broken prayer were lost.

That was not the last meeting by the side of the little brook where Ered had often lain to tell her trials, to listen to the plash of the water on the stones, and to dream of the country she had never known. Between these vague longings, these yearnings and herself, there rose a figure more real and definite; though when she was alone her thoughts shrank fearfully from this Estri of a land that was not the country of her vows. And still they met, though as if by accident, and he whispered words of reverence and sympathy. The Estri, still simple-hearted as a child, could only express his love by reverence.

Meanwhile, the winter passed, and through all the Fair Country alarm spread as rapidly as a kindled fire; and in every mouth through the whole length of the land could be heard the names of the country's enemies. Ascar, like others, had become aware of danger, had taken his place for the first time as Councillor, had listened to the message from the Maravel of the Rema, and had shared in the terror with which it was received. It was the first time that he had been absent from his home, and he was full of the pride of his new dignity; but still through all feelings, like a golden thread, ran the remembrance of the Nira slave. His companion, Olbri, returned from a hunting expedition, had soon discovered the existence of a secret, but with the proud reserve peculiar to him, would not attempt to penetrate the mystery. The Estri only observed that his companion was pallid—and in those days every man knew anxiety.

A crisis followed. On a night of shivering moonlight Ascar stopped at a shepherd's hut to ask for milk ; and, entering the hovel after he had secured his horse, became aware of a stream of gold upon the ground. As he stopped in confusion it slowly raised itself, and by the light of the solitary torch he saw Ered's face—tear-stained, with the haggard, terror-struck expression of one who has passed through dread experiences. Between her convulsive sobs he heard her tale—a slave had revealed their meetings to her mistress ; she had been seized, and threatened with the scourge, until, freed by her desperate struggles, she had rushed out into the night. And now, weeping bitterly, she cried out to Ascar that she must set out at once to find her country—she had vowed to devote herself to her country and its gods—but before she could complete her sentence he had clasped her in his arms. That first, only kiss remained as a spell with Ascar when he was once more on the moonlit plain. One vision possessed him with overmastering power—the beautiful fugitive should be his bride.

A dangerous resolve ! but the Lord of the Escola, strong with his first, mad dream of happiness, could not pause for a moment and attempt to estimate

the strength of superstition in the land or in his
bride. With the aid of his rank and wealth he
swept obstacles away. An old debt had placed
Ered's mistress in his power; and the other
Estria, harassed by the war, could not offer a
determined resistance to his will. Whilst hurried
wedding preparations were being made, the bride
was sheltered by the shepherd and his wife, who
were always present during Ascar's daily visit, for
Ascar still treated her with the utmost reverence.
That she was remorseful, terrified, in agony, dread-
ing alike the gods of his country and her own,
that the vehemence of his love repelled whilst it
overwhelmed her, was knowledge Ascar had never
realised. As little did he know that, seated by
his side, Ered longed in anguish to start up before the company, and pouring out passionately
her remorse, her fears for him, declare to them
all that she would not be his wife. Her
limbs quivered, the lights swam before her eyes,
weights held her down, starts of agony oppressed
her; and Ascar reclined by her side, absorbed in
bliss, in the triumph of the hope on which he had
staked his life. Let the enemy come! for in the
future evil days he would have the memory of his
wedding-night.

Olbri, meanwhile, was silent, as he had been
silent on the evening when he stood with his
friend on the platform of the Escola; when, as

they looked out on the moonlit, shadowed hills, Ascar confided at last his dearest hope. Ascar did not know that the bruised hand he saw next morning had been passionately dashed on the rock the night before ; his friend only seemed to him silent and disdainful, and the Estri was not sure that he had been even interested. Yet Olbri could still see the moonlit, shadowed hills as he had once seen them through a storm of tears. He must submit ; it was of no use to struggle, although this wedding should destroy not only his friendship but his friend.

And so, pale, quiet, clad in unornamented green, he sat behind Ascar at the wedding-feast, listening to the music, to the rising storm, observing the movements of the company. It was the first time that he had seen Ascar's bride, the bride of whose beauty he had heard so much—she was certainly beautiful—but it was strange that she never turned her face towards her husband. Ah ! ah ! it was possible that Estri Ascar might not gain unmixed happiness with his Nira slave—and then love and gratitude cried in sharp reproach that he was exulting in his friend's destruction. At the moment he winced before this lash of shame, the unseen chorus broke out again in song, and for the instant its triumphant outburst subdued every other sound to melody.

Torches are shining, and music is ringing,
  Soon will the marriage bread gladly be broken,
Soon will be silenced the voice of our singing,
  Soon in the stillness the promise be spoken.
Come to the bridal !   Though spirits of sorrow drear
  Many a knot on the sad earth can sever,
We need not tremble, nor dread the to-morrow here.
  Come to the marriage feast !   Love is forever.

Is love forever, slave and nobleman ?   Is it
impossible for love to die ?   For one instant dark
visions rose again round Olbri ; to fling them away
he started to his feet.   The music had ceased, and
through the wedding-hall there swept only the
sounds of wind and conversation.   As the wizard's
son moved, every eye was drawn towards him, but
he had determined to surprise the company.

I I.

What is this world's delight?
Lightning that mocks the night.

Comes a vapour from the margin, blackening over
    heath and holt,
Cramming all the blast before it, in its breast a
    thunderbolt.

IT was the moment for speeches, but the guests
had not supposed that the opportunity would
be seized by the wizard's son. As the friend of
the bridegroom, however, Olbri was not without
protection, and in Ascar's presence none dared
to hinder him. Without any sign of fear he
walked boldly to the table, and took up a goblet,
which he filled with wine; then moved behind the
empty carved seat at the left hand of the bridegroom, and stood still, resting his arms upon its
back. His pale eyes, his inexplicable manner,
the absolute uncertainty what he would do or say,
held the company with a momentary amazement
which only gave place to more intense surprise.

VOL. I.   C

The burning words might be from the wizard's son, but the chord that was struck was one which thrilled them all. Breathless, amazed, without looking at each other, the guests were silent, all eyes being fixed on him.

'All hail! I drink health to the Rema, our visitors! I drink health to the men who come armed to take our land!

'Fellow-guests, you and I are visitors to-night at the bridal-feast of the Lord of the Escola. There is no greater joy, say our poets, than the bridal. Estri Ascar is generous; he shares his joy with us. But Ascar—*Estri* Ascar, generous-hearted as he is, has not so many gifts as the Rema can bestow. They will give us chains, fire, ravished wives and murdered children, cruel masters to carry us to a bitter slavery. These are their gifts, and you will agree with me that even the intention of them deserves reward. We will reward them indeed with the best recompense—the best. To these Rema bridegrooms we will give a wedding-feast.

'Look round you to-morrow. Beneath this guardian rock lie the meadows of our beautiful land, the bride they claim, decked with white blossoms as for a festival, a summer garment that may serve for her bridal robe. We, too, will put on the best raiment that we have, and with our sharpest swords we will go out to meet the bridegrooms. There will be shouting then, a mighty clamour—

believe me, my friends, it will be a blithe marriage day.

' But every marriage-day passes into evening, even as we meet here to-night at Estri Ascar's wedding-feast—and on this day of the Bridal of the Rema, on this great day also the end will come at last. And *then*, when the torch is dim, the shouting over, when the bridegrooms, pale with delight, have claimed their brides, *then* the earth, drinking in their blood as her marriage wine, will take their bodies to her embrace.

' To the Bridal-Feast of the Rema ! '

He tossed off the wine in his goblet at a draught, flung it over his shoulder so that it fell with a loud crash, and sat down. And as he did so, moved by one common impulse, the guests in the wedding-hall started to their feet. Touched by fire, for an instant they could not remember that the words they heard had been from the wizard's son.

A tumult followed. The men who were present drew their swords, and struck them together after the manner of the Alidrah—a noise that was mingled with the shrieks of some of the women, terrified at the blades which were crossed in front of them. Ascar had risen, and with quivering pulse, and a glance alight with flame, stood as master of the tumult. Ered, with pale face and wide-opened eyes, sat as in a dream, looking on the company. But Olbri, meanwhile—Olbri had flung himself into

his seat, pale, excited, but yet with lips that seemed
to smile ; the low, sneering murmur trembling on
them almost audibly,—

'A fine speech for the son of the sorcerer!'

And now above the shouts, 'To the Bridal of the
Rema,' rose the chorus of the unseen singers, and
the shouting died away.   For singers, as the nearest
approach to the voices of the Akbare, commanded
reverence in the Alidrah.

> Come to the marriage-feast ! Over the mountain's side,
>   Flapping its wing, the slow death-bird is flying.
> Come to the marriage-feast ! Down by the river's side
>   Spirits weave shrouds for the dead and the dying.
> Did they not promise us on some to-morrow drear
>   From our loved homes and our children to sever?
> Why do they lie then in silence and sorrow here?
>   Come to the marriage-feast ! Death is for ever.

Is death for ever?   Then tenfold woe to the
guests who shout so triumphantly at Ascar's wedding-feast!   For invaders are advancing as a torrent on the land, and a few empty boasts will not
be sufficient to resist them.   It may be that, as the
excitement slowly died, some consciousness of un-
spoken dread possessed the guests.   But before the
reaction of feeling could be shown, a second current
rose with another speaker.

He was an old man, and his brown robe (though
it was thread-bare) proclaimed him a Councillor of
Neridah, especially as there shone upon its breast
the yellow jewel only Councillors can wear.   His

white hair, his trembling hands, and feeble manner, made a contrast to the appearance of the son of Olloto; and the guests, at once silent and intent on hearing, evidently rendered an accustomed reverence. The first words came faintly; they appeared to rebuke the company for forgetting even to mention the most hated enemy—and then suddenly, with his head flung back, and old eyes blazing, he poured out his sentences with the strength and fire of youth. No fanciful eloquence of metaphor was here, but the force of a bitter hatred gave enough intensity.

'Death to the Exiles! Death to the sons of those whom we drove from our country! Death to their leader! May an evil star rise over them! May their names be forgotten! May their bones whiten our land! They come to us with multitudes. They bring the fiends themselves against us. They believe that we shall bend as weak reeds before their will. In silence let us call on them the Curse of the Akbare. To the sorcerer leader and the men who follow him!'

He spoke, and crossed his old hands upon his jewel, and the men who were present crossed their hands upon their swords—in another instant it seemed as if a spell were resting upon the bridal company. Before long the silence became unnatural; but no one could break it, and it still lasted on; until in itself it was painful, terrible, a

weight of oppression under which none dared to
breathe. And still it was held—when suddenly
a curtain rustled, a messenger entered the Hall of
the Escola ; and in an instant, with a sound low as
a sigh, a single universal movement stirred the
guests. They were not left without another cause
for dread, for the Estri followed the messenger from
the hall. It must be some grave reason which
in this sudden fashion could call Estri Ascar from
his wedding-feast.

All tongues were loosened. And since minds
were turned to Alvo, it was natural that the young
leader should inspire them—the more so, since the
phantoms which had gathered round his name
made fanciful horrors, fit for a wedding-night. His
marvellous beauty was mentioned — the women
shuddered, and were interested ; his physical
feebleness—the men displayed contempt ; the blood
which he drank to support his failing health, his
nightly spells for the assistance of the demons.
The Hall of the Escola was full of conversation
when a curtain moved, and the bridegroom entered
it. In another instant, when his face was visible,
a silence of breathless terror filled the place.

Ascar stood in the midst. His face was pale,
his dark eyes fixed ; the young handsome bridegroom was transformed as by a spell. Once,
twice, he attempted, he tried in vain to speak,
and each time his trembling mouth refused the

words. And then the words came, and fell into deepest silence, the silence of a terror more piercing than suspense. Motionless, rigid, with hanging arms and parted lips, the bride sat silent, with her blank eyes turned to him.

'A message from the Estria. Without the delay of another instant I must attend the trial of the Governor of Neridah. The truce is broken. We may expect the approach of Ursan. And the Nira —the Nira take part with the enemy.'

There was silence. With wide-opened eyes the bride started from her seat—scarcely conscious, panting, quivering from head to foot; whilst Ascar, with a face of hunger and despair, strode up to her to give his last embrace. All heard her wild cry, saw her repulse him with her hands, and saw that he seized her with an iron grasp; that he crushed kisses on her, and with fierce, broken words commanded her to await his return to the Escola. As he released her, and she fell back, almost fainting, he turned away abruptly, as if he could bear no more, flung orders to his servants, signed to Olbri to follow him, and strode through the midst of the guests, and from the Hall. Behind him were lights, confusion, the trembling, awe-struck company, the disordered banquet, the silent instruments and minstrels—the whole spectacle surging in one tumult in his brain as he passed the threshold and went out into darkness. His hope had touched him and it was torn from him like the torn roses which he flung upon the ground. In a frenzy of mingled rebellion and despair he left the banquet and strode out into the night.

III.

What a bridal night is this ! . . .
Laden with the chill of death
Is its breath.

A something light as air—a look,
A word unkind or wrongly taken—
Oh, love that tempests never shook,
A breath—a touch like this hath shaken !

THEY went together down the dark path, Ascar
and Olbri, the path which led to the foot of the
Escola, weird now with shadows of overhanging
branches, though moonlight shone upon the great
plain below. The familiar scene and the familiar
companion, the cold air of the night-time and its
solitude, were strange as a dream after the heat,
lights, and clamour, the music, the madness of the
wedding-feast. But Ascar was still hot with wine
and disappointment, jarred from head to foot by
anxiety and grief, unable to console himself even
by repeating passionately that before the next
sunset he would be with his bride again. He had
not forgotten that, at the moment of their parting,
Ered had tried to thrust back his embrace. He

was angry with her, troubled that he should be angry, appalled at the darkness which was closing round their lives. Sore with irritation, he could scarcely bear the silence, and yet was not pleased when his companion spoke. For the first time it occurred to him that the wizard's son should show respect when he addressed a nobleman.

'The Estri is on foot,' said Olbri, accustomed to reprove his friend, 'when he should have taken with him horses, arms and men. Thou art so disdainful, Ascar, of the most ordinary precautions; thy valour needs a background of experience.'

'I return to-morrow,' answered Ascar, haughtily, 'so there can be no need for me to surround myself with an army. My own horse is lame, and I will ride no other; and, moreover, on these rocky paths I prefer to be on foot. If we are attacked I have, at any rate, my sword; and, besides, thou art with me, if that counts for anything.'

'It may count for something,' Olbri answered, lightly, although the words had not been spoken as a jest. 'But a creature who is not an Estri must not venture to pretend that he has the valour of the Estria.'

It was evident that the wizard's son was not respectful. The Estri had been too indulgent. . . . Then, ashamed of the moment's thought, stung with a sense that he was being ungrateful, Ascar spoke with more quickness and less haughtily.

At that moment they had reached the foot of the
Escola, and could see the great plain, and the stars
above the plain.

'I hoped that the Governor of Neridah had
escaped,' he said, with a manner and voice more
like his own. 'He is an old man, and his
daughters are beautiful — everywhere they are
called the Roses of the Alidrah. At one time
I fancied that I loved one of them, and for her
sake I still wish well to her father. But the new
Governor accuses him of being Alvo's friend, and, if
that is true, he deserves the punishment of death.'

Olbri did not answer at once. Ascar had
observed before that he paused at any mention
of the accused Governor's name. Then he said
lightly,—

'Ah, Alvo, the blood-drinker. No man who
loves wine should call himself his friend. The
sorcerer Alvo, I feel drawn to him. The sorcerer's
son should meet the sorcerer!'

He had spoken lightly, but Ascar turned towards him with such anger as he had never displayed before.

'Thou jestest at everything,' he cried with fury,
'at every enemy, every peril of the land! It is no
wonder that thou are called a traitor, and that I
am accused of being a traitor's friend. The husband of a Nira! That might be forgiven, but I
shall not be forgiven for companionship with thee!'

Even as they fell, he would have recalled the words, but they were spoken, and there was no escape. Olbri did not answer, and in silence they passed from the shadow of the rock to the moonlight on the plain.

The silence, the starlight, had rebukes for Ascar, but he was still heated, beyond measure tempest tossed, more ready to justify his conduct to himself than to humiliate himself by penitence. Was it for Olbri to be injured, to be sullen—Olbri, for whom he had sacrificed so much? And yet, as a quick, light touch saved him as he stumbled, Ascar felt once more the reproach of ingratitude. But he could not speak, and his companion fell behind him; it seemed easier to be silent a little while. Youth is soon sorry, but it is sure of life, and counts on opportunities.

Olbri, meanwhile, was saying, as he lingered more and more, with sadness rather than anger in his heart,—

'So it has come the time of separation, though I did not think Ascar's lips would tell me so. But I will stay with him till he has joined his comrades, it may be the last service I can offer him.'

They went on in silence along the rough paths, beneath the light of the moon, and the radiance of the stars.

And now a shout greeted them from a band of figures, who were, like themselves, on the way to

Neridah—foot soldiers, summoned to attend the Governor's trial, and delighted to have Estri Ascar's company. Their leader, a stalwart captain, who knew the young Estri, whispered apart to Ascar that he had some fear of an attack—it was said that a band of Rema were concealed in the neighbourhood—he was glad to observe that the Estri had a sword! The reproof was good-humoured, and restored Ascar to good-humour, whilst the prospect of danger was exhilarating—his dark eyes were shining with their accustomed eagerness when he turned round to summon Olbri to his side. But Olbri was gone, and during a few minutes it was impossible to discover what was become of him. The leader was impatient, but Ascar would not move; his compunction did not allow him to part in this manner from his friend.

It appeared at length that the wizard's son had left a message; he had gone back to find a gold charm which he had lost, and when he had found it, or had given up the search, he would come on alone to Neridah and would join the Estri there. Ascar was uneasy, although relieved by the message, which he felt was intended to give him that relief—he did not like to leave his companion alone, almost unarmed, exposed to all dangers of the night. But he had been summoned to the Governor's trial, and was under necessity to reach the town before dawn; and, moreover, Olbri was always quick and skilful, much more apt in any time of peril than himself. He yielded, therefore, reluctantly, to the will of Bere, the leader, and permitted the little band to resume its march, with the inward promise that when he met his friend he would be gracious and they would not dispute again. Ah, fool, in such times of danger to count on the morrow's sun, even after the experience of the wedding-feast! Full of fancies and dreams he scarcely saw the wood they entered, the dark trees that shut the stars away.

And then, in an instant—he had not time to think—he knew they were surrounded, he heard the clash of arms; he saw the gleam made by torches in the darkness, and wild savage faces on every side of him. He struck out fiercely, but his blows struck trees and air; it was dark, he was confused, he knew not what he did; he received a blow on the temple, his sword fell from his hands, he felt himself falling, as if he were sinking through the night. And then, when, confused, with aching eyes and head, he struggled, as one in a dream, to get to his feet, he became aware that his movements were impeded, and then that both hands and feet were bound with cords. As he struggled to a reclining position all slowly became clear—distinct as a fiery dream in the night's darkness.

They were in the wood; there were torches, lan-

terns near them; on all sides his comrades lay upon
the ground; above them stood dark men with long
gleaming knives, which they raised at each motion
that the captives made. Near Ascar, with blood
streaming from his wounded side, lay a handsome
lad who had known the young Estri well, who had
served often as his attendant in the hunt, in the
pleasant familiarity of such companionship. He
looked up now with a smile in his dark eyes, as
he became aware of the presence of the nobleman.

'A bad day for *us*, Estri Ascar,' he whispered
below his breath, at once exhausted by his attempt
to speak.

Ascar could not answer, for some men laid hold
of him, and dragged him roughly over the uneven
ground. Once more for a while he found himself
bewildered as if he were sinking through unfathomable darkness.

He recovered to hear the sound of angry voices,
and to be conscious that men were disputing over
him—two men who seemed to be leaders from the
richness of their dress, and from the authority of
their manner and words. They were violently angry,
and their voices rose and fell in the fierce grating
accents of the Rema tongue; but Ascar, although
he had learned the Rema language, listened long
in vain before he could distinguish words. He
was only able to catch at last one sentence—a shrill,
screamed sentence from the man who turned away.

'The Leopard shall know of it, the Leopard shall know!' he cried. 'It shall be worse in the end, Corlon, for thy prisoner and for thee!'

His glance dwelt on Ascar with malignant hatred before, turning to his men, he addressed some words to them. In an instant all knives were unsheathed with many jests, the mirth of men who have congenial work to do. And in the same instant the meaning flashed on Ascar —the prisoners were doomed, the prisoners would be killed!

He had no time for thought. He was roughly told to rise. The man that had been called Corlon appeared to take charge of him. He was placed in the midst of a little band of men who, without any delay, prepared to leave the wood. There was only one moment—one instant's awful knowledge of torches, lanterns, and long knives red with blood, of low groans uttered by the wounded and dying, of dark forms bending over them to strike again. His head swam, his knees trembled,—sight and knowledge deserted him ; for some instants he remained insensible. He was moving, and there were others moving near him ; that single faint consciousness was all he had.

And then—he was standing upon a bare hillside, with Corlon near him, and the little band of men, and a few horses tied to the olive-trees, misty as shadows in the grey light of the dawn. His hands, feet were bound ; he was a helpless captive ; dark, cruel faces were on every side of him ; far away in the distance, over the great plain, the first signs of morning were breaking through the darkness. The wedding-night was over.

THE CAPTIVITY OF ESTRI ASCAR.

Ad perennis vitæ fontem mens sitivit arida,
Claustra carnis præsto frangi clausa quærit anima,
Gliscit, ambit, electatur, exul frui patria.

I V.

ASCAR stood, bewildered, in the light of the early
morning, whilst the sky flushed rapidly with the
crimson of the sunrise, for the first time able to
think, to realise the tremendous change that had
overwhelmed his life. It was all over, his comrades
had been killed ; he was bound, a prisoner, in the
hands of enemies. For the first instant it was only
possible to be sensible of absolute astonishment.
But the Rema were masters who were well disposed
to give their captives enough to think about.

'Take that for thy pretty face, Estri,' said Corlon
as he passed him, dealing him a buffet with the
greatest possible good-will—so that for the first
time Ascar understood that the pleasure of striking
makes some men give blows. The Rema laughed
loudly, and seemed to be as pleased as if they had
been hearing some well-flavoured jest ; with the
greatest good-humour then gathered round their

53

leader that they might receive instructions for the day. Ascar stood apart, and blood rose to his face, burning it with the sense of shame and indignity. His feet were bound, and he would make no effort to escape which might give them an excuse for insulting him.

Ah! during those instants what bitter yearnings rose for Ered, Olbri, from whom he was separated now; and what would he not have given to remember that he had parted from each with tenderness? It was almost a relief to be roused from such remorse by the men who closed round him as his body-guard, although in a moment he became aware that he would have to endure fresh suffering—the position of the insect which sees around it those who are strong to hurt helplessness, and to whom the sight of pain is sport!

'Hola, Estri,' cried one, in the language of the Alidrah, though with the vilest accent in which any tongue could speak, 'we are set to watch thee while the others have their meal, and it is only fitting that we should have some sport. Thou shalt sing, shalt run, shalt dance for us, little Estri, or we will prick thee with our swords, or lay a scourge across thy back. Run now. Thou wilt move so gracefully with our cords at thy heels. I tell thee, run, or it shall be worse for thee.'

With a sinking at the heart which made his

blood feel cold, Ascar realised that it would be
worse for him; but what Estri of the Alidrah
taught an Estri's pride, could resign himself to obey
such commands as these? He remained still,
self-angry for inward shuddering, and was then
dragged, struck, and kicked by his body-guard
and at last thrown over, and beaten with the most
vigorous stripes that his captors could inflict.
Perhaps the fear had been worse than the pain,
for he was not unused to hardships, though the
adventures of the chase had not prepared him for
such torments; he mustered patience and endured
his chastisement until he was allowed to rise to his
feet. Stiff, irritated, with each nerve in a rage,
he had now to endure the amusement of the band.
And yet these men must have been bred on mother's
milk, these fiends who had no pity for his sufferings!

'Let the Estri alone, Nardi,' cried Corlon from
a distance, where he sat squatted above his morning meal; 'he shall fast while we eat, and as soon
as we have done he shall learn to run until he can
run fast enough.'

Ascar heard the men crying that Maravel Corlon
knew—he would give the Estri a lesson when the
morning meal was over; and then they all threw
themselves down to eat and rest, leaving him to
remain standing near them, breakfastless. Sick,
angry, ashamed, and hard-pressed with despair,

Ascar could not think even of his friend or of his
bride. He stood gazing helplessly over the wide
plain, the vast extent from which no help came to
him.   The Spirits were angry, they had been
angry with his marriage, they left him to be in
the hands of his enemies. He could not pray to
them, although he longed to pray ; he was in-
vaded by a dark sense of punishment. Ah ! if
he could not reach the Akbare—the Spirits of
the Earth—how much less the Silence . . . where
the gods live . . .

And now the short meal was over, the horses
were untied—there were only a few horses for the
band of men—and, whilst preparations were being
made for departure, the dark-faced leader came up
to him. By his side was another man who was
taller, slenderer, and who gazed at Ascar with
cold, observing eyes—himself also a leader, as was
evident by the gold brooch, the Rema sign of
authority. He appeared to address some advice
to the other Maravel, which Corlon received with
the utmost impatience and disdain, turning away
to call the men to bring his horse, and to attach
the prisoner to the saddle with a cord. Ascar
could not understand Corlon when he spoke to
him, though the words were supposed to be uttered
in the language of the Alidrah ; but as the Maravel
mounted and the horse began to move, he grasped
with one shock of terror the nature of his punish-

ment.   One instant's experience of sickening,
mortal dread, then one vain effort to keep pace
with the steed, and then he was dragged over the
uneven ground, with darkness and flashes of fire
in his brain and eyes.   And then all was over . . .
he was lying on the ground . . . he could see dark
faces between him and the sky.   Terror and suffering alike were past ; he was in the condition that
is beyond the reach of pain.

The other leader, whom the men seemed to call
Iscar, had checked Corlon's horse by his hand
upon its rein, and now dismounted, with severe,
scornful words, that he might examine the condition of the captive.   It was by his orders, or it
appeared to be, that Ascar found himself lifted
from the ground, his wounds bandaged, and his
hair drenched with water, while his lips were
wetted with some rough kind of wine.   Even
these attentions, however, could not entirely revive him ; his limbs were powerless, and his head
was faint ; he was only conscious that after a
while they bound his eyes, and that he was laid
upon the back of a horse.   Weak, weak to helplessness, and burned with fever, he knew no more
on that day, or for many days.   No more—he
had a haunting dream that he was being always
carried onwards, but beyond that sensation his
mind was powerless.

It passed, however, after a while, the time of

fever, the indescribable oppression which tor-
mented him, the sensation of being carried to
some unknown country, where he would be left
in darkness, lost for ever.   He began to recover,
to hear the voices of the Rema, and even to relish
the food and wine they gave, to be aware that his
wounds were healing, and to know when he was
laid on the ground and his bandages were changed.
And then that time also passed into heavy sleep—
the reaction by which nature recruits itself—and
in one or two more days he was sensible that the
tide of young life flowed in his veins again.   The
next day, in the early morning, after a night of
broken rest, he heard a halt called, and was lifted
from his horse.   The bandage was taken from his
eyes; and, with a sharp, penetrating thrill, he
wondered if he had been brought to some lonely
place to die.

This was what he saw as he stood with trembling
eyelids, oppressed even by the light of the rising
sun—the great plain round him, and immediately
in front of him a solitary rock which reared itself
above the plain.   Iscar was gone, and most of the
men were gone—there were only left Corlon, a few
on horseback like their leader, and one or two
who had dismounted, and were laying hold of him
that they might place him with his back to the
rock.   Still confused, he became aware that near
him were iron rings, and that fetters were being

fastened to his wrists; then that with these he was attached to the rings on each side of him so that it was scarcely possible to move. They would kill him now! but they did not try to kill him, they stood in front of him, and laughed out in his face; they mounted their horses, and shouted words of greeting, and waved their arms in the action of farewell. Bewildered, convinced that they intended to kill him, he could not understand that they were going away; not even when he saw that their horses' heads were turned, and that their dark faces were grinning back at him. In another instant his dazed eyes followed them as with swift movements they swept across the plain—they were gone, they were lost, and he was left alone, with his back to the rock, in the midst of solitude. There was not a sign of any human being; hê stood there with fettered hands—he was alone.

V.

Who wickedly is wise, or madly brave,
Is but the more a fool, the more a knave.

AND, meanwhile, upon Ascar's fatal wedding-
night, Maravel Rudol had lingered in the wood
that he might arrange the division of the plunder
after Corlon had departed with the young nobleman. There was not much plunder, however, to
be found on the dead bodies—on the leader was a
gold ring, on another man a purse; these were the
only valuable prizes, and these Rudol claimed,
without hesitation, for himself. The men dared
not complain, for they observed their leader's
scowl, his thin lips twitching, his hands playing
with his sword; they had never seen him so angry
since the days when Maravel Alvo lived in Ursan's
camp.

'He will hate Corlon,' they whispered to each
other, 'as he hates the young leader.'

It was now time to leave the wood, for they might
be surprised from Neridah; though, as they num-

bered forty men, they were not much afraid. One
valiant soldier had a notion of his own,—

'Why should we not go on and take the town?'

'Remove his plunder for speaking,' the leader
growled, and pointed to his own heap, upon which
it was laid forthwith.

No one ventured to complain of this command
—the mood of Maravel Rudol demanded obedience. And it went ill with any man who offended
Rudol, for he was the favourite of the old Maravel.

Not a beauty although a favourite! since even
the wavering light of torches could not soften the
defects of this leader's face and form, which might
have justified the opinion of the Alidrah concerning
the appearance of its enemies. The eyes of Rudol
were small, his features ill-set and crooked, his
forehead so low as to be almost imperceptible—
for which reasons his men called him the 'Delight
of Eyes' whenever he was not likely to be near
enough to hear. A dangerous title! but the
tongues of Rema soldiers cared little for danger
when they indulged their venom.

'What story will he carry to the Leopard
now?' they whispered. 'The wretched Corlon
will be torn limb from limb.'

'All the same, he need not have claimed our
prisoner. That prisoner was a nobleman. His
chain was valuable.'

'What does it matter to us if it was valuable?

Maravel Rudol would have taken it. Corlon is a
fiend, but he lets his men have plunder. And
Maravel Alvo—he is generous.'

The sun was rising as these words were said,
and they looked down from a hill-side on the
wood which they had left. One solitary figure
was hastening towards it; it was Olbri, upon
his way to Neridah. The men would have been
willing to return and chase him, but they dared
not speak to their leader, who was already far in
front; and meanwhile Olbri, unconscious of danger or calamity, entered the dark wood, and was
lost to view. The Rema, unseen, hastened to
rejoin their leader; and pursued their way un-
molested until they reached Ursan's camp.

In a few days they reached it. They had
travelled northwards, keeping under the hills to
the left of the great plain. The journey had been
rough, and they were all disheartened because of
the small amount of plunder they had gained.
Rudol, for his part, had his own cause for fury,
as he urged his horse restlessly over the rocky
paths. It should go ill with Corlon if he could
compass his revenge, and yet it was not of Corlon
that he thought.

It is possible for a great love to make us churlish,
from our wish to keep all our affection for one
object of desire; and in like manner a great hatred
can absorb our bitterness, so that we shall grudge

the wrath that another object claims. Whatever feelings of malice entered Rudol turned to one object as the rivers to the sea; they were fresh items in one long reckoning which should yet be visited on the young leader's head. With this perpetual sensation in his heart, not less burning because of its present helplessness, in the hot light of a summer's afternoon, with his men behind him, he entered Ursan's camp.

They had turned to the hills before they reached the camp, and had wandered amongst the rocky ways for hours, until they crossed the Tordrade which leaps and sparkles there, reserving its solemnity for the plain below. They crossed the stream not far from the Varidi *(water's music)*, the beautiful waterfall loved by the mountain-tribes, pleasant to see and hear with its rushing, driven foam, before entering on the brawls and licence of the camp. Rudol stood on the rough bridge, and gazed into the water—after stumbling, and glancing covertly to see if there were any smiles; but in all the beauty of the rushing foam and torrent he saw but one object—the young leader's face. A beautiful face! he saw it in the dust, and himself at last able to place his foot on it.

The camp, which they entered now, was in a nook amongst the hills, and had been for many reasons selected by the *Leopard* (thus named on account of an animal, sent from a distant land,

with whom Ursan had been reared in childhood;
or so at least tradition said). The place was
difficult to attack, and easy to defend, not far from
the Alidrah, and close to the mountain-tribes, with
some of whom the Maravel was conducting nego-
tiations which would enable him to move forward
without danger at his rear. And yet, in spite of
these advantages, the Rema soldiers wondered
that their leader allowed them to remain in idle-
ness; and some of them imagined secret ways and
counsels, and waited for further events to supply
the information they desired. They were used to
secrecy; not one of Ursan's leaders could fathom
the schemes of the old Maravel.

The blaze of noonday was on the camp when
they entered it; but the heat had not affected the
spirits of its occupants, to judge by the uproar
which rose from every side. The sound of the
rushing Varidi was lost in coarse jests, loud
laughter, the rattle of drinking-cups, the clamour
of rude singing, angry words, and fighting, all
mingled in indescribable uproar. A camp of
extraordinary licence! in which, at first sight, it
appeared as if each man governed himself without
fear of a ruling power; for only a long acquaintance
could reveal the complete control exercised by the
Maravel. It was in this manner, through permitted
evil, that the Leopard preferred to make his power
felt; uproar and licence did not trouble him so

long as his soldiers were obedient. And indeed
they obeyed him most implicitly; they said 'It
was better to obey than to be torn;' and every
experience confirmed the knowledge that they
had ample reason to dread their Maravel. To this
statement, however, it should in honesty be added
that they rendered him at the same time their
supremest love; their inexplicable, treacherous,
terrible old leader was the one man they thought
worthy of 'a place among the gods.' He had
the crown of success; since he had been their
Leader-King he had never failed to lead them to
victory.

And now Rudol stood in the camp in deep
reflection, already beginning to feel some thrills of
fear, and to doubt whether it were safe to seek the
dreaded Maravel with angry complaints of an
action ordered by himself. His men lay about on
the ground, drank wine, and watched him with
furtive glances that did not betray their thoughts,
though it is difficult to conceal hostility from an
irritable and jealous consciousness. Once Rudol
turned on them, but, accustomed to the movement,
he could only see them lying with their wine-cups
by their sides; and it was not until he disappeared
among the tents that their laughter and foul
epithets broke out unrestrained. Rudol did not
hear them, he had other work to do; already he
had entered the tent of the Maravel.

No other man in the camp durst have entered there unsummoned, but this leader had the privileges of an acknowledged favourite, although the conflict between dread and fury in his breast was displayed in the hesitation of his steps. As he entered he started like a criminal on hearing himself greeted by his leader's voice. Soft tones had that voice, but to those familiar with Ursan the strangest thoughts were recalled by its harmony.

'Welcome, Rudol,' now murmured its gracious, mellow accents. 'Come, sit at my feet. I was expecting thee.' And Rudol advanced and bent his head and knee without raising his glance to meet his leader's eyes.

Ursan was seated upon a bale of goods, with another and larger bale behind his back, above him hanging the lamp by whose aid he wrote at night, or held midnight consultations with the leaders of his troops. He had been leaning forward with his head upon his hand, and the expression of one who is lost, absorbed in thought; but as Rudol entered, he slowly raised himself, and his grey eyes became keen, as if they had been lit within. Rudol felt their glance, but dared not raise his own. Rent with fear and anger he found words impossible. His leader appeared to like the sight of his discomfort, and enjoyed it in silence for a while before he spoke.

'Ah, was thine expedition successful?' Ursan

asked, in one of the smoothest tones of his soft voice.

Rudol made with his hand a motion of assent. He knew that he was being played with, and would not deign to speak. Rudol was not brave, but on this particular occasion his wrath enabled him to be unusually courageous. For the first time he was conscious of some degree of strength, although in the presence of the Maravel.

As for Ursan, he smiled, but the smile only added hardness to a mouth which was harder because its lips were full. His gracious tones continued murmuring, evidently he intended to amuse himself. If the Leopard were more dangerous at one time than another, it was on such occasions of apparent playfulness.   •

'Did Corlon meet thee? I sent him after thee. Did he claim a prisoner when the fight was over? Unfortunate Rudol!' and once more Ursan smiled.

Rudol was silent, stung by the mockery.

'Were there any gold chains amongst thy prisoners, Rudol?'

'There was one, Maravel.'

'Corlon claimed it, I suppose?'

Rudol was silent. Ursan looked at him more keenly.

'And what was he like, this man with the gold chain?'

'I know not, Maravel,' in slow, sullen tones.

'He was young, dark, a nobleman, and a councillor.

'Young? Ah, ah, thou hast really gained a treasure! Thou hast done me a service, dear Rudol. It was the Evil Star himself! Thou art astonished, but I have studied the Estria. Hast thou never heard of Ascar of the Escola? Thou art always ignorant,' said Ursan, as his companion did not answer. 'He is the head of the noblest family in the land. We will burn his home soon, and kiss his Nira bride. Were the others all slain as I commanded?'

'All—but one, Maravel.'

With the eyes of Ursan on him, Rudol dared not speak anything but truth. A long experience had taught him that with this terrible commander truth was invariably the safest policy. He did not cease to think so, although the change in Ursan's face warned him that his answer had not been satisfactory.

'And where was that one?' Ursan asked. 'Did he escape? Did I not give an order that the whole band should be killed? Are my orders disobeyed?'

Beneath the smoothness of his tone could be heard the fierceness of the old tiger-cat.

'Who was this fellow? If thou hast let an Estri slip, I shall not find it an easy task to pardon thee.'

'He was not with the others. . . the prisoners spoke of him. . . .'

Rudol faltered, for his anger had become absorbed in fear.

'They called him—Olbri.'

As he pronounced the word, Ursan's brows relaxed, and he leaned back, more satisfied.

'Ah! Olbri!' he said. 'The son of the sorcerer. The Evil Star's hated companion. We may leave him to his countrymen.'

'What dost thou not know, Maravel?' Rudol cried with admiration.

A smile from Ursan rewarded the compliment.

'I have good spies,' he said, in a deprecating tone. 'Well, I forgive thee. So thou hast been angry with me?'

Rudol was silent.

'My Rudol can be angry. He ought to be wiser. Although he is most wise.' Ursan's sentences fell like stings, but his question was less mocking. 'Will he bring his wisdom to the council in my tent to-night?'

'If the Maravel please.'

'It is as my Rudol please. I can then send him to plunder the Agra. Will Rudol plunder?'

'If the Maravel please,' replied Rudol, but this time his tone was eager.

Ursan laughed softly. His voice became so gentle that it had the effect of a caress.

'See that you burn every home—but thou
wouldst do that for thine own pleasure. Give the
women to the soldiers, and throw the children in
the fire. Wilt thou take my share of the plunder
in exchange for thy nobleman? I claim half the
plunder. Ah! that pleases thee.'

Rudol was pleased indeed, for this proof of his
leader's favour would have the effect of a poisoned
sword on Corlon. With a relieved mind, and an
anger half allayed, he dared at length to look at
the Maravel. And Ursan from his bale of goods
glanced down on him with eyes that seemed full of
thoughts which he would not express in words.

'Sit down and talk. I will listen to thee and be
idle,' he murmured in the sweet, lazy tones which
he could command at will. 'The Varidi is not
more musical than the sound of my Rudol's voice.'

My Rudol's voice was of the harshest, most grating nature, but this circumstance increased the
compliment. He squatted eagerly down upon the
ground—an acknowledged spy who had always
much to tell. But whilst he poured out his store
of petty news, deeply tinged with his own rivalries
and enmities, Ursan, though listening to him attentively, listened with eyes that were looking far
away. He made no comment when the information was exhausted; and, after a moment's silence,
Rudol rose.

'Ah, why so hasty?' asked the Maravel, raising

his head. 'There are still some matters on which
I must speak with thee. I have news to tell thee
of thy lost nobleman. Sit down. I have listened,
and thou must listen too.

Rudol sat down, with some visible reluctance;
but Ursan even then would not speak, but leaned
forward, lost in thought—an expression which
made his face seem worn and aged, though it had
still firm features beneath hair streaked with grey.
The favourite had become impatient of the silence
before the old Maravel raised his head at last.
Ursan spoke in a low and in a different tone; he
took no trouble to make his voice sound gentle
now.

'I have heard,' he said, 'from the young leader.'

Colour flew into Rudol's face, but he only bent
his head. Ursan glanced at him before he spoke
again.

'A long message—for Maravel Alvo.'

Rudol bent his head once more.

'His camp is in order, the Effar are satisfied. I
shall never again find a leader who governs men
as Alvo does!'

There was silence.

'That was not all,' Ursan said in a lower tone.

Rudol raised his face with a strange, wild gleam
of hope.

'Alvo hears—certain rumours.'

'Certain rumours,' Rudol muttered.

'Relating to *Me*. He asks me to explain them.'

There could now be no doubt that the Maravel's tone was sinister, and Rudol's heart choked him with eagerness.

'He has heard that I intend to make the Alidrah a province of the Rema.'

'Ah,' said Rudol.

He could think of nothing else to say.

'That I shall have massacres in this Alidrah— he is never satisfied with my massacres. He is afraid that I shall destroy his country—he loves his country so much, our little Alvo.'

A pause followed, for Rudol did not think it safe to speak. One feeling—only one feeling— grasped his heart.

'So Alvo has dared the Leopard's teeth at last!'

'It was a respectful message,' Ursan said. Thou mightest learn courtesy from Alvo, Rudol.'

'I had rather be rude and honest, Rudol muttered.

'Learn honesty then,' said Ursan; and he smiled.

But Rudol for once did not heed him. He was excited, trembling, scarcely able to keep still upon the ground. His eyes were full of a vision of his enemy close, close to a monster who was ready for a spring.

'Alvo has dared the Leopard's teeth at last. Alvo is so hasty. I knew—I knew he would!'

'Hast thou, Maravel—?' he cried with excitement, and then stopped.

Ursan turned towards him the cold gaze of his eyes.

'Have I answered the message?'

'Ah, truly, Maravel.'

'What else should I do? I answered yesterday.'

'And—'

'Thou would'st ask what I said? I said some words about the Effar. I praised my son Alvo. I promised to send him money. I said that it delighted me to hear from him.'

'And—Maravel—'

'Thou would'st ask what else I said? I told Alvo he should not pay heed to idle rumours. I said we would laugh over these stories when we met. What is the matter?'—for Rudol gasped for breath.

'Your wisdom, Maravel, is great. I dare not say—'

'It is *thy* wisdom I have asked to hear.'

Rudol paused to collect strength.

I should have told him,' he cried out, 'that I allowed no man to write such words to me! I should have called him insolent, presumptuous, an upstart, and have warned him that he must prepare for punishment.'

His vindictiveness choked him this time, not his terror; he became silent from necessity.

'Wisdom!' cried Ursan. 'The skilful, crafty Rudol! When I wish that a man should follow me I must begin by striking him! My little son Alvo is the best of all my tools; I am to rouse him against myself, and then break him for my pains! Thou art a fool, Rudol!'.

Rudol answered sullenly,—

'I have not the wisdom of the Maravel.'

'It is prudently spoken.' Ursan's voice was scornful. 'Still, do not be angry, Rudol; come and listen near my mouth. Instead of permitting Alvo to declare that I have wronged him, I would force him to confess that he has injured me. Your wisdom, Rudol; how shall I manage that?'

And Rudol's face became bright, though he did not answer for a while.

'I would set spies to listen to his words.'

'Ah! Ah! Thou rememberest those capricious words. But he never speaks against me; and, if he did, who would care? Once more!'

'I would send men to his camp to raise a riot.'

'They will find it hard to do that in the camp which Alvo rules.'

'I would wait—till he had committed some error—'

'That might be to wait long.'

Rudol was silent, though his face showed eagerness.

'Thou hast no answer? Listen, then, my foolish

one. Two of Alvo's nobles are amongst these mountain-tribes. I learned so much from the Sena who brought this message to me. Alvo is too wise to trust his own men in my camp. Rudol, no leader may take another's prisoner. That is a law which even these barbarians own. The injured leader may choose his own amends. Wilt thou now forgive me for stealing thy nobleman?

'Thou art silent. Listen. These men have openly declared that they will release any prisoner left to starve. This Evil Star is our prey. We will chain him to the Essil, the rock on the great plain which these men must pass. They will pass by, will release him, be detected. I shall have been injured, will avenge my injury. Thou art not satisfied?'

'The men may not pass that way.'

'Ah, dost thou think I should leave that to accident? The Effar, my spies, will entice them to the place. The Rema will watch, and take them with their prisoner. Ah! thou art smiling now. What pleases thee?'

'Maravel,' asked Rudol, bluntly, 'what will thou do with the men?'

'They shall go to the Leopard's Den. I will not have them in the camp.'

'And then—thou wilt write to Alvo?'

'I have already written to him.'

There was silence again, and the face of Rudol

fell. But Ursan's voice broke the pause in softest
tones.

'Why should I quarrel with my son, my little
Alvo? It will be easy for me not to have heard
of the dispute. In these times of conflict there is
much that is not heard ; or I may have sent to tell
Alvo, and have lost my messengers. These men—
favourites—shall be my hostages. They will be in
my hands to do with them what I please. I can
make them the means of treaty if I will, or I can
make them the means of punishment.'

Once more there was silence. Ursan seemed
lost in thought ; but the small eyes of Rudol were
bright with inward triumph. Ah ! Alvo was close
—close to the Leopard's teeth.

'Alvo is so fiery. This scheme will ruin him.'

'When Alvo knows—' he said, almost unconsciously. And Ursan raised his head as if he had
been roused from sleep. 'When Alvo knows—'

'Rudol, it is almost night. Art thou not tired?
Go to thy tent and rest.'

Rudol was accustomed to such abrupt dismissal.
He saluted his master at once, and turned away,
observing that Ursan scarcely heeded him, as he
sat bent, crouching, with his head upon his hands.
A deep abstraction ! But it did not much alarm
the man who knew his master, and his master's
favourite. The old Maravel might wish to delay
an outbreak, but he would never baulk himself of a

scheme so congenial. And the brother-leader, with a nature like a flame— Ah! there was no fear that he would not destroy himself.

'Alvo will find the Leopard's teeth sharp when they are meeting in his neck,' Rudol thought, as he walked through the clamour of the camp.

Leaving that camp to its open, secret evil, we will seek justice in the Fair Country.

And, moreover, I saw under the sun the place of
judgment, that wickedness was there ; and the
place of righteousness, that iniquity was there.

ON the morning that succeeded the wedding-night
of Estri Ascar the members of the Council of
Neridah were assembled, still keeping the anxious
watch which they had maintained through the
long hours of the night. Caution was needful—
outside was the tread of crowds who had slowly
collected round the Council Hall, keeping their
own watch through the stormy night, whilst the
Councillors waited silently within. There was
grandeur in the dim vision of this multitude of
men, pressed together, with sombre faces, with
weapons in their hands—a great force holding
itself in check, until the moment for energy should
come. Now and then there were tremulous movements through the mass which pressed it together
more closely than before ; now and then low
murmurs, the murmur of many people, which

reached, like some sound of waters, within the
Hall. But the movements ceased, and the murmurs died away; the moon waned, the night
passed, there came the faint light of the dawn;
and, as if with that light the need for restraint
were over, the voices rose again, with greater
freedom.

'He will come soon,' they said; and then, 'We
hear him coming;' and then, as that hope proved
vain, 'They will bring him soon.'

And then the murmurs swelled into angry
voices, as if surging waves were rising round the
Hall.

'Why do not they bring him?'

'They are fooling us; they do not mean to have
a trial.'

'They are afraid.'

'If they are, it is the first time I have known
Maro fear.'

'Is *he* in there?'

'They say he will kill the Lord Governor.'

'Then they say what is false, for we will save
him.'

The members of the Council heard the shouts,
and looked on each other. But the crowd went
on talking.

'They say he knew Alvo.'

'He never did know Alvo.'

'They say he confessed it with his own lips.'

'It is false.　He never confessed it.'

The voices became more and more angry.

'Why are they waiting?'

'They must be afraid.'

'They are waiting for the Estri of the Escola.'

'And where is the Estri of the Escola?'

'Oh,' replied one, with a sneer and a shrug, 'Estri Ascar will not be in a hurry, he is keeping his wedding-night.'

'He is a good man, is he not, Estri Ascar?'

'He must be, since he chooses this time to marry a slave.'

'Marry a slave!'

The crowd became excited.

'What better could he do?　She is not worse than his friend the sorcerer.　Estri Ascar is a happy man, between a sorcerer and a witch!'

'Burn the witch!'

'And the sorcerer!'

'They say he will bring his friend with him to-night.'

'Then we will tear him in pieces.'

'You are wrong in one thing,' said a man.　'The lad is not a sorcerer, he is only a sorcerer's son.'

'It is all the same.'

More murmurs, more restless movement, then another outbreak,—

'Why do they not *begin*?'

'Is Estri Envar in there?'

'Yes, truly, he is the Iltro.'

'What does *he* come here for?'

'Because of his love for the Governor's daughter,' one man sneered.

'Did he love her?'

'No, he did not.'

'Yes, he did.'

'We will break open the doors if they do not begin.'

So cried the crowd, becoming more impatient every moment.

And, meanwhile, the unseen Councillors watched and waited anxiously.

It is certain that no two men do the same thing in the same way. The waiting Councillors had their points of difference. Some were quiet, some restless, some evidently terrified; some, in spite of anxiety, overcome with sleep. The most noteworthy in appearance, a tall, dark man, sat perfectly upright, with his chin on his clenched hand—a hand so tightly clenched that it seemed to tell of a passion which was not in his face. This man was Maro, Lord Governor of Neridah.

In the centre of the Inner Hall was the carved seat of the Iltro, or judge. Here rested (for his eyes were closed, although he moved restlessly) a fair-haired, slender young man, with a gold chain round his neck. He was Estri Envar, one of the principal Estria, who had been summoned from the South to attend the Council. Some said that he was himself under a shadow of suspicion, and that for this reason he had been made the judge.

The lamps had been extinguished as the pale light of morning entered ; it was already more than time for the trial to begin. Outside the doors could be heard the impatience of the crowd.

' The Estri of the Escola does not seem disposed to come,' Maro muttered, with some impatience in his tone. ' Estri Envar ! '

Envar opened his eyes wearily.

' Would it not be well to have the doors unbarred ? '

' I cannot tell,' Envar answered, with a long weary yawn. ' Is not Estri Ascar coming ? '

' He does not come.'

' Poor fellow, he is married,' mumbled a fat, sleepy man, who awoke to make this remark, and then went to sleep again.

' And the first result of his marriage,' spluttered a choleric little creature, ' is that his Nira witch-bride keeps him away from the Council.'

' He had better be punished then.'

' Why not punish her ? '

' Fie ! fie ! ' from a third. ' No talk of hurting women.'

'And why not,' asked the Governor of Neridah, *since they hurt us?*'

He seemed to glance at the Iltro from the corners of his eyes. There was an uncomfortable silence.

Envar threw himself back in his carved seat. His face was throbbing with the blood that had risen to it.

'Why do we not begin?' he asked with fierce impatience, as if he were ready to find some excuse for wrath.

'We are ready, Estri,' answered the Governor, quietly.

'Give the orders then, Maro.'

The Estri spoke with haughtiness, but the Governor would not seem to notice his ill-humour. When he had given the order, he leaned over Envar's chair.

'It is necessary to admit the crowd. I have commanded, in consequence, that all guards should be doubled. You are willing, I trust?'

'I have not thought about it,' Envar yawned.

There was some visible contempt in Maro's glance. The young nobleman observed it, and it roused his perversity.

'It will be better to wait for Estri Ascar.'

'I think not,' murmured the Governor, with his usual quietness—a calm that proceeded from a decided mind—for Estri Ascar was considered a

friend of the late Governor, and Maro had determined on the late Governor's death.

'We do not need more than one Estri,'—he
appealed to Envar's vanity. 'The Estri of the
Escola is not indispensable.'

'He is insolent not to obey our summons,' Envar
muttered. 'But he was always a fool.'

'I thought him talented.'

In reality, Envar admired Ascar, and Maro considered him a fool; but it was natural for one to
exalt, and the other to depreciate a nobleman.
There was no time for any further conversation,
for preparations were being made for the trial to
begin. The members of the Council arranged themselves in a semi-circle, indicated by a black line on
the pavement of the Inner Hall. The Governor of
Neridah alone continued standing, leaning upon
the back of Envar's chair.

'We must make an attempt to escape a riot,' he
said. 'That would be dangerous—with the Rema
close at hand.'

'Are they so close then?'

'It is in the air.'

He could say no more, for at that instant the
doors were opened; and immediately the Hall became filled with multitudes.

Pressed together, a heaving, sullen mass, on all
sides could be seen the lowering brows of men.

'What guards could protect us if these should

rush on us to save him?' whispered Envar, with a thrill that was irresistible.

'True,' answered the Governor, with his keen gaze on the crowd; 'but they hate Alvo, and that hate is his destruction.'

Envar answered with a thrill of another kind of fear—this trial was more terrible than he had imagined. Doubtless, if he could have foreseen his sufferings, he would not have been so ready to sit in judgment on his friend.

And now the sound of a disturbance in the distance made it evident that the prisoner came at last. The tramp of guards could be heard, the soldiers' voices; and then from all sides rose shouts of welcome.

'Health, Lord Governor! We are all here to protect you.'

'May all good spirits bless him! He saved my child.'

'He saved *me*.'

'We are your guards, Lord Governor. Do not fear.'

'Listen to their insolence,' muttered Envar; but Maro only smiled.

The guards forced their way through the Hall, and drew near the Iltro's seat. And now before the young Iltro stood the prisoner, with each wrist chained to a guard on each side of him. The crowd looked at him, but the Council looked at

Envar, who was unable to preserve absolute composure. When he had last seen this man whom
he must judge, he had received from him a father's
tenderness.

The prisoner was an old man, with an upright
figure, and the expression of one long accustomed
to command. One careless, proud glance he cast
round the crowded Hall; then saluted the Council
with simple dignity. Then he gazed at Envar
with a scrutinising glance, as if he were looking on
him for the first time. Envar became pale, though
he had before been flushed; his pride had a pang
from this indifference. But he who consents to sit
in judgment on his friend is well advised if he
prepares himself for pangs.

'Nart Uvrode,' said Envar, with his usual grace,
which did not desert him even in this agitating
moment, 'you come here under a heavy accusation. If you are condemned—you will be liable—
to the severest penalties.'

'To death,' said the Governor, quietly, as he
stood behind Envar's chair.

With equal calmness the prisoner looked at him.
But the word was followed in an instant by an
uproar, whose irresistible clamour filled the Hall.
Uvrode turned quietly to the Iltro's seat, and
craved permission to speak to the populace. It
was not granted, but he took silence for consent;
and, turning, addressed himself to the multitude

His clear, calm tones fell like water upon fire ; but through them spoke an indefinable sadness.

'Good people, kind friends, I thank you for your pity. But in a few moments you will cease to care for me. Till then, be silent.'

And as fire hisses, is extinguished, there followed one surging movement — then a silence, intense as death. Calmly, as one who has fulfilled his duty, the prisoner turned to the Iltro's seat.

'Are you my judge ?'

'Why should I not be your judge ?'

'You are young,' said Uvrode, smiling, 'to judge an old man. I am ready.'

Envar's face had flushed with rage ; there was no hesitation in his manner now.

'You are accused, Nart Uvrode, of having eaten bread with Alvo.'

There was a moment's silence.

'*It is true.*'

As the words were uttered, a low sound like a groan trembled through the multitudes in the Council Hall. A sudden light darted into Maro's eyes ; for in that murmur he heard the doom of death.

'I have known Alvo.'

'In battle ?' Envar asked, disdainfully.

'No, Estri ; when I last fought for my country Alvo was a boy, as you were then.'

The young Iltro was checked ; but Maro took

the word, apparently unable to veil his eagerness.

'You are doubtless aware, Nart Uvrode,' he said,
speaking with distinctness, 'that no man may eat
with the enemy of his country.'

His manner was sinister, but no uproar followed.
The old man met his glance, looking steadily at
him.

'It is necessary that I should explain myself.
Four years ago we were in the land of the Ar-Nira.
The mountain-tribes attacked us, and our home
was burned. We were in danger. A young
leader came—'

'You mean, *Alvo* came,' the Governor interrupted.

'*Alvo*—though that name meant nothing then.
He saved my life, and protected my daughters
from insult, remaining with us that he might
guard us more securely. He fell ill. We took
care of him. He was very ill. It may be—it is
possible—that our care saved his life.'

A low, sullen murmur ran through the crowd,
and in sudden triumph Maro bent to Envar's
chair.

'That is his death-warrant,' he whispered ; but
Envar's lips were white, and he would not raise
his head.

Maro turned to Uvrode, and the two men
looked at each other with the steady glances of

powerful dispositions. There was no personal resentment in one face or the other, even in these instants of a conflict unto death.

'Ah! so—' said the Governor, whilst his right hand stroked his beard — 'it is owing to your attention that this Alvo's life is saved?'

'It may be so,' Uvrode answered, quietly.

And the crowd listened in a silence like despair.

'You do not repent; you would save his life again?'

'I know him now to be the enemy of my country. Even then, though I loved him, though he had saved my life, I thought him a man whose faults would ruin him.'

'And yet you loved him?' Maro's voice rose like a hiss. 'And your pretty daughters?' •

'How dare you speak of them?'

'Your pretty daughters love Alvo, it is said.'

Uvrode glanced at him, then turned desperately away.

'*You know my daughters*, Lord Iltro,' he cried out, in his voice the sound of a desperate appeal.

A sensation of danger rushed to Envar's heart. With an instinctive movement he turned away his head. And then for the first time the prisoner lost his self-command; his hands clenched, and all could see him grind his teeth. Only for a moment; he rallied all his strength, and in another instant his face was calm again.

It was at this time that there rose a sudden
clamour; cries, groans, even shrieks pierced from
without the Hall; and the tumult without was
answered by excitement, for in those days of peril
crowds were quick to catch alarm. Ursan was
come! they were all dead men already! A
quivering motion passed through them, as of
flight. But the Hall was so crowded that flight
itself was impossible.

'Calm yourselves,' said Maro, drawing himself
up to his height. 'Retain your places. I will
send a messenger.' Then, remembering that he
was not the Iltro, 'You will send a messenger?'
he whispered to Envar.

Envar glanced at him peevishly, turned his
face away, and moved his shoulders, and then
sent a messenger. It was impossible not to feel
the bitterness of possessing the name of power
without its reality.

The messenger went, returned, and with a face
as pale as death forced his way once more through
the excited people. With the same absorbed look,
as if he could scarcely see, he stood before the
Iltro, and saluted him.

'The Estri of the Escola, and the others summoned to the Council, are lying dead in the wood
outside the town.'

Through the whole Hall there rang a sudden cry,
as if every man in the multitude was doomed

'Who brought the news?' cried Envar.

'Erv Olbri, the sorcerer.'

'How did he know?'

'He was with them in the fight.'

'And how did he escape?' asked Maro, suddenly. 'He is wounded, at least?'

'He is unhurt, Lord Governor.'

The ugliest smile crept into Maro's eyes. He glanced at Envar, who spoke immediately.

'Let Erv Olbri be brought,' commanded the young Iltro. And then, in some doubt, he looked at the prisoner.

'Ah, let him wait a few days,' Maro cried. 'We must find these beautiful daughters, that they also may be punished.'

Uvrode trembled visibly, but he only said,—

'I think that you have no daughters, Lord Governor.'

For one instant Maro turned pale. He had a daughter, but years before she had left her father's home. And instinctively, at the sight of that sign of pain, Uvrode murmured on the instant's impulse, 'Pardon me.' His words were not heeded, the pang of old remembrance had only for an instant pierced the Governor. Already he was dreaming of another victim, who should make the crowd eager by a taste of blood.

'Listen,' he whispered to Envar; 'we must hear this Olbri's story, though the town is fortified,

and we need not fear. There is one advantage
to be gained, at any rate. The son of the sorcerer
is in our hands at last.'

Envar looked at him, but could not understand
the expression of triumph which had risen on his
face. For himself, he was trembling, unable to
recover from the sudden tidings of Estri Ascar's
death.

Possibly even to Maro that news was a bewilderment, but the Governor would not allow himself
to dwell on it; one moment's thought he had
given to the condition of the town, and then had
returned to his immediate design. He had not
deceived himself; the crowd had been gloomy, not
excited; his rival had still a hold on its affection;
but this new terror—this old hatred of the wizard
—if only he were permitted to conduct this trial
himself. For some instants he meditated, with his
hand clenched on his mouth, whilst a commotion
of exclamations and inquiries filled the Hall. And
then, with a manner of excessive deference, and
yet full of resolution, he bent to Envar's chair.

They whispered; the multitude was restless; the
guards pressed it back by force; Uvrode kept
his eyes on the Iltro and the Governor—the grace-
ful youth whom he had once loved as a son, the
rival who had stolen his Governership. What
were they plotting, these men who cared for
power; and who, as it seemed to him, loved

nothing else? What was Maro plotting, whilst Envar moved and twitched, and the Governor bent on him a face, pale, inflexible? The prisoner sighed; he was a man of steadfast nature, but even his steadfastness yielded to despair. Was another victim to be sacrificed to the ambition of these men, whilst justice—lived in the White Heaven, not on earth?

And now—fresh commotion, fresh clamour from the crowd announced the approach of the son of the sorcerer; and Envar peevishly turned his face away, whilst Maro drew himself up with gleaming eyes. Whatever their dispute had been, it was obvious that he had triumphed. He stood still, resolute, with his lips pressed on each other; and Uvrode, observing the expression of his mouth, muttered to himself with a thrill,—' That face means death.'

Ah! poor, reckless lad, no longer sheltered by an Estri. . . At this moment the crowd parted, and the face of Olbri could be seen. The intent gaze of multitudes was fixed upon it—this second examination would be even more exciting than the first.

Olbri entered slowly, and his blank, fixed eyes gave his face an expression none had seen it wear before; it was evident that he had no consciousness of danger, since he made no affectation of his usual audacity. His appearance created an impression in his favour, and the murmurs which had greeted his entrance died away. The crowd closed upon him ; surrounded on all sides, he stood before the Iltro, and saluted him.

'Is this dreadful news true, Erv Olbri?' Envar asked, and the other Councillors poured out bewildered questions.

Olbri answered faintly ; he had still the look of one who has received a shock from which he cannot rouse himself.

'It is true, Estri,' he said ; and then, shivering, he paused for an instant before he could speak again.

'In the early morning I found the bodies in the wood ; they were lying there, but the enemy was gone.'

'And—Estri Ascar?'

'I do not know.'

'*You do not know?*'

'I searched for him,' said Olbri, shivering again. 'The bodies were stripped, gashed—it was difficult to be certain ; but I believe that I did not find him there. He may be alive.'

His tone of eagerness was pathetic. It said,— 'Do not take my last hope away.'

The Councillors broke in with questions ; but his answers were impatient ; and at the first pause he addressed his entreaty to the Iltro.

'I have brought the news here. And now let me depart that I may join those who are pursuing the enemy. Estri Ascar may be alive.'

He was already turning away, when a glance

from Maro rested on the Iltro for an instant. If the vanity of the Estri were wounded by that summons, Envar did not—perhaps he dared not —delay to respond to it.

' Not yet, Erv Olbri,' he said.

' Ah, let me go ! '

Olbri was almost in tears, which he restrained with difficulty. Without even waiting for an answer, he turned away.

'Come back to your place, Erv Olbri,' said Envar, quietly — the quietness through which speaks authority.

Olbri turned round, surprised, but still suspecting nothing ; at that moment he could only be conscious of the danger of his friend.

' As I have known you, Erv Olbri, and your friend, Estri Ascar, I leave your examination to a more impartial judge. You are under suspicion, and must submit to trial. I resign my seat to the Governor of Neridah.'

Envar said the words gracefully, and they were greeted with applause—at that moment he felt almost contented with himself. He rose with the grace of one who performs a voluntary action, and Maro came forward to the carved seat of the Iltro. Olbri was roused by an unexpected thrill ; and yet, even then, he was scarcely sensible of fear. Only, as the Governor looked on him with cold, fixed eyes, rose the thought, ' I have no Ascar to defend me now.'

'You were with the rest of the band before the battle, Erv Olbri?' Maro asked.

'Not with them. I did not choose to walk with them.'

'Not with Estri Ascar?'

'Estri Ascar was with the leader.'

There was some audible bitterness in Olbri's tone.

'But you were with the others?'

'Only for an instant. I went back to find this charm—this gold bee—which I had lost.'

'Is it possible that you hoped to find so small a thing?'

'I found it.'

'And then—'

'I tried another path, and lost my way.'

'All the paths here should be familiar to you.'

'But they are not.'

His breast heaved indignantly. The Governor smiled, as if he enjoyed his questions.

'You found the right path, I suppose—when the fight was over?'

'I did,' said Olbri.

'Are you brave?'

Olbri was silent.

'You do not answer me.'

'*How can I answer?*'

At this moment the crowd howled, 'Coward.' Olbri smiled.

'Is it not true, Erv Olbri, that you have said a man who dies for his country—is a fool?'

'I said so in jest,' said Olbri. But he coloured now with shame.

'You have said that the Rema are as good as the people of the Alidrah?'

'I said that in jest.'

'You have said many things in jest? Is it in jest that you imagine yourself brave?'

Olbri was silent.

'Or that you did not flee from the Rema?'

'I did not flee from the Rema.'

'Do you think we believe you?'

Olbri was silent.

'It is for you to speak,' said Maro. 'Defend yourself, or be ready for your doom.'

There was breathless stillness to hear the prisoner's words. Olbri saw eager faces on every side of him. They wished him to be condemned, they were amusing themselves with him. No one would believe him. What was the use of words?

'I have nothing to say,' he answered, sullenly. But at sight of the Iltro's smile he bit his lips. 'If Estri Ascar were here—'

'Could he help you if he were?'

'Oh,' cried Olbri, appealing suddenly and passionately to the young nobleman, '*you know me, Estri Envar!* Do you believe me a coward? Speak!'

It was the voice of a man pleading for his life, whom the word of an Estri could declare guiltless. The colour of Envar came and went. Without meeting the prisoner's eyes he turned away his face. After all, what did he know, and why was he called upon to place himself in peril for the son of the sorcerer?

'I know nothing in your favour,' he muttered, below his breath.

And the crowd broke once more into delighted cries of 'Coward!' 'Coward!' murmured also a voice that no one heeded. The old man was not thinking of the son of Olloto.

Olbri crossed his arms on his breast. He knew now that he must collect his courage; that there was no refuge between him and his doom. An erect, slight figure, he stood before the Council, with the silence of one who is prepared for his fate. Yet, young as he was, it was hard to repress all agitation, but his crossed arms concealed the beating of his heart. On every side of him were the hard eyes of the multitude. He would not give way before so many enemies.

And now, after the Councillors had whispered, Maro rose, and turned an unfathomable gaze on the prisoner—a cruel pause, prolonged with the intention of straining the prisoner's courage to the utmost. Olbri did not break down; he was steady, resolute, meeting the eyes of the Iltro with an unflinching stare. But he knew that his pulses were beating feverishly, and that their rapidity drove the blood from his lips. After all, the suspense could not endure for ever. The interval of silence passed, and Maro spoke.

'Erv Olbri, you are pronounced a traitor and a coward, and you must prepare for a coward's punishment.'

'Oh, kill me at once,' muttered Olbri ; and the low, hoarse voice seemed to the listening multitudes a cry of pain.

'We put brave men to death,' answered the Iltro, with contempt. 'You are sentenced to be branded, and then banished from the country. You may go to the Rema, to the camps of Ursan and Alvo. Your father's country is not in need of you.'

'Ah, sorcerer !' cried the crowd. 'How do you feel now, sorcerer ? '

But Olbri turned to them with his usual audacity.

'Wise countrymen,' he said, 'you have good rulers who, to satisfy you, sentence men whom they *know*—'

'Be silent,' interrupted Envar, his lips quivering with rage.

'Silence,' echoed the Governor, 'or you will be whipped as well as branded.'

In spite of this threat, Olbri would have spoken further, but a good-natured guard laid a hand upon his mouth.

'The sorcerer's son is worthy of his father,' Maro said. 'Your father's name will be even more dishonoured now.'

Olbri looked at him, but only muttered,—

'You are cruel.'

The Iltro went on speaking, to the enjoyment of the crowd.

'You will be branded in the face,' he said, 'that all men may know your sentence. The beauties of the Alidrah will not regret you after that.'

'You would not taunt me,' muttered Olbri, beside himself, 'if you had courage, if you were yourself a man. And *you*—'

He turned to Envar with a scorn too great for words.

'Twenty lashes for that,' said Envar, quietly.

He was surprised that the sentence came easily, for he was merciful.

'Good ones, too,' echoed the Governor, laughing loudly. 'Let him be guarded till the evening, and then—'

'And then he will be punished,' Envar said.

'Some day, young Estri,' muttered Olbri, 'you also may know what punishment is like.'

The words were heard only by Uvrode, who, on being led away, had turned to lay a kind hand upon the young man's arm. But Olbri saw in the motion only a movement of rejection, and an old remembrance increased the pang. With the words,

'I can bear it no longer,' in his heart, he turned to the guards and said abruptly,—

'Let us go.'

Through the clamouring multitude he passed with a firm step. The voices of opposition gave him courage. But when he found himself in an empty chamber, his head became dizzy, and he staggered to the wall. One of the guards turned to clap him on the shoulder, and to assure him that 'it would not hurt very much.' The little kindness had almost overcome him, but even when he was left alone he would not weep.

No, he was tired and faint, but he was also angry, bitter; and, flinging down the gold bee, he crushed it with his foot, although then, in swift penitence, he raised and fondled it, because 'it was punished for nothing, like himself.' He must not be weak . . . and, lying down upon the ground, he covered his face with his hands, and tried to rest; tried in vain, for there still rose innumerable faces, whilst the sounds of echoing tumult filled his ears. What would become of him? He had lost his friend, his father; all love, all memory were swept away; even the father's name, which he had shielded, was turned into dishonour now and shamed through him. The fire which had been kindled in his heart was checked for the time by the dull tide of despair. Motionless, without stirring limbs or features, he lay with his face hidden, waiting for the rest.

VII.

The way to the stars.

THE rest followed in due course. On the succeeding evening—that is, on the first night of Estri
Ascar's captivity—the Nuldah, Ascar's head huntsman, lingering in the courtyard of the Escola,
heard a low signal, which he knew, beyond the
wall. Without answering, he stood still, in the
attitude of one who listens, who is startled, for
rumour had brought tidings of the son of the
sorcerer.

It was a hot, still night. The tower of the Escola
was dark ; the few stars flickered with a faint light
in the sky ; and round the moon was that dim,
lurid halo supposed by the people of the Alidrah
to show the 'spirits' wrath.' And yet the old man
had lingered in the courtyard, whispering to himself that Estri Ascar might return—Estri Ascar
was so strong, he might even yet come back,
having saved himself from the hands of his enemies.

In vain! the courtyard was silent, until now, through the stormy night, there came the echo of a familiar sound. Once, twice, the low cry was repeated; and then, slowly, noiselessly, a figure dropped over the wall, and stood within. At least it was not the hand of Ascar's servant which opened the door to the son of the sorcerer.

The old man stood, motionless, in the moonlight, with his hand on his hunting-knife. Olbri remained, motionless, against the wall. He was so still that, on that weird, stormy night, the image seemed more like his phantom than himself. The thought crossed the huntsman's mind, but before he had realised its terror, the figure before him advanced some steps, then stood still. It *was* the son of Olloto . . . and the old man experienced àn overwhelming sensation of mingled horror and triumph.

'Why hast thou come to us?' he cried out sharply.

And the figure answered,—

'Am I a stranger, then?'

The words were in the tone of Olbri, but his attitude was not like himself, for he seemed ready to sink with pain and weariness. Slowly, as if he were afraid of falling, he let himself drop upon a block of stone. But even in that instant he kept his head erect; and the old man, standing in front, looked down on him. A keen, slow gaze as if,

standing there in the moonlight, he were drinking
his fill of a long-delayed retribution.

'Ah! they have branded thee!'

'They have branded me,' said Olbri.

'And they have beaten thee?'

'They have beaten me.   Thank the gods.'

He turned up his face with his usual mocking
look; but the next instant it was bent, shaken by
a storm of sobs.   With a different terror the old
man bent over him, and by grasping his shoulders
saved him from falling.

'Have they hurt thee so much then?'

'No—I am a coward.'

'I thought thou wert brave, Erv Olbri.'

'I tell thee, I am a coward.   They have given
me the name to wear, and I will wear it—on my
face, on my heart, till I return to the Alidrah.'

'Till thou return?'

'Oh, I shall return,' said Olbri.   'When I have
found the way to the stars, I will return.'

'Art thou mad?'

'No, old Nuldah, I have been mad all my life.
And now they have shown me how to reach the
stars.   For the sake of my father, of Ascar, I have
been virtuous, and they have beaten and branded
me to teach me better.   I have learned from them.
When I return to the Alidrah they will be compelled to own that the stars bend to me.'

'Thou art certainly mad.'

'Wait and see.' His laugh was harsh. 'I shall win the Fair Country for my father and myself. Dost thou think I shall endure this mark upon my face—I, who am my father's son, and have been Estri Ascar's friend?'

His voice failed as it fell into gentler accents—his head bent, and for a while he said no more. Then,—

'Fetch me thy Estra.'

'What is Estri Ascar's bride to thee?'

'Thou hast said the words. She is Estri Ascar's bride.'

'And what wouldst thou do with the Nira who has ruined him, who should be offered to the gods to save his life? Ah! who could deliver our Estri when the Akbare were angry because he had linked himself with a slave and sorcerer?'

'Fetch the slave!' cried Olbri. 'Tell her the sorcerer is waiting! Art thou deaf? Fetch thy Estra. I vow by all the fiends that I have not come here in vain to seek Estri Ascar's bride. I am risking my life each moment that I stay. But I will see Estri Ascar's bride before I go.'

The old man looked at him, and seeing that he was resolute, departed slowly, muttering to himself; his indistinct words mingling spells against the demons with imprecations on Estri Ascar's enemies. Olbri remained, unheeding; and leaning on the wall, looked down upon the wide country, dim with night, save where here and there some stream, touched by the moonlight, shone like a thread of silver in the gloom. The scene of a dream! in which he himself was a phantom, lingering for an instant in familiar haunts . . . He turned as he heard the sound of footsteps—there, standing in the moonlight, was Estri Ascar's bride.

Her figure was distinct in the moonlight. She was in rough slave's attire; upon her bare feet were sandals, and there were steel rings round her ankles, her only other ornament being the beautiful hair which fell over her shoulders, almost to her feet. Seeing her thus altered, and only for the second time, it might have been difficult even to recognise her, if the expression of her troubled face had not recalled the scene of the wedding-night. For, changed as she was, and though her eyes were dull with the look of one who has been entirely stunned, her lips, still quivering with inward conflict, preserved their expression of anguish and hesitation. She stood there with her head bent, in slave's attitude; and Olbri left the wall, and came close to her.

'Do you know me, Estra?'

She raised her eyes to him with the dread of one who is surrounded by enemies, and yet with something of the imploring look of one who dares not lose the remotest chance of help. Even from the midst of his own misery, Olbri could feel the loneliness of her position. His tone was softened beyond its usual wont in his attempt to be compassionate.

'They have told you—I am Olbri, who was Estri Ascar's friend. I have been branded. I must leave the land to-night. I have come to see you . . . We have only a few instants. I want to offer you all the help I have . . . Indeed, you may trust me. I have not been false to Ascar. I would have died to save him. It is for his sake I come to you.'

As she still looked at him he held out both his hands; and slowly, mechanically, she placed her own in them. And then, as she felt his grasp with its assurance of protection, her fixed look melted into a rain of tears. Instinct warned Olbri that it was best to let her weep; he stood still, holding her hands which clung to his. The scene of the wedding was with him; it seemed only in a dream that he stood in the moonlight with Estri Ascar's bride.

Ered cried,—

'Help me. Tell me what to do. I am afraid of them. They will kill me. I cannot help myself.'

She looked into his face with eyes large with tears and dread.

'The Spirits are angry; they will not speak to me.'

'The Spirits!' echoed Olbri, with a gleam of his mocking smile.

She saw it, and dropped her hands, but she still looked up at him.

'Oh, I believe in the Akbare; I have believed in them. I have broken my promises, and they punish me!'

'I will tell you'—she yielded to the instinct of confession. 'When I was a slave I was often left alone; and I used to lie in the long grass by the stream that I might be near the Spirits of the Water. And I used to promise the gods in the White Heaven — the gods of the Nira—that I would belong only to my country. I vowed to find it—and then Estri Ascar came; and I—I was frightened'—her words were broken by her sobs. 'And then — the wedding-feast — I was afraid to speak to him. . . . I could not go back and be a slave again. . . . I longed to marry him, but I felt the gods were angry, and I kept fearing that I should ruin him. . . . And now they are angry, I have made them angry with Ascar — and I cannot help him, and his servants wish to kill me. I am alone. I am frightened. Tell me what I ought to do. I am afraid they will kill me. I am *afraid!*—'

'Your gods do not help you, Estra?' murmured Olbri, speaking gently.

'Tell me what to do.'

'I know nothing of the gods. How are you treated?'

She trembled.

'They sent for me when I awoke—when they first heard the news, before I heard the news—I thought they would kill me, but the Nuldah drove them away—and then he looked at me, and I was afraid of him! He said that it was possible the gods might need a sacrifice; he put out his hand, and I feared that he would kill me! And I shrieked, and he despised me. He said I was a coward and a slave. He said that the gods would despise such a sacrifice! I could have been brave then, but he would not hear me; he told them to bring my slave's dress, and to guard me in my room. . . . I used to think I could do the will of the gods when I lay in the long grass by the river's side.'

'Ah, Estra,' said Olbri, 'concern not thyself with the gods. Have they helped thee? Did they come to the aid of Ascar? I am wiser than thou, for I expect no help from them. Listen, Estra. This morning I was condemned, being innocent; this evening I was led out before the multitudes, and whilst they howled with delight I was whipped with ox-sinews, and then branded with a hot iron on the face. Was there one, Estra, only *One* from the Unseen, to come forward and say, "I will help the innocent?" No! From

this time I heed neither gods nor men. But I
will do one thing for my honour, even if I die
for it.'

He paused, a peculiar expression stirred his lips.
He muttered,—

'The son of the sorcerer should meet the
sorcerer.'

Ered looked at him timidly. He repeated
aloud,—

'The son of the sorcerer should meet the
sorcerer.'

'What is that?' she murmured.

'Some words I said to Ascar—Estra, I have
only another moment with thee.'

'Art thou going?' cried Ered, in sudden misery.
'And then I shall have no friend in all the world.'

'No friend but the wizard?' cried Olbri; 'how
can I accompany thee, with this mark on my
face so that all men see my shame? I am banished, cursed; I dare not even look for Ascar, for
my help would call on him the curse of gods and
men. No. I must leave thee. One present I can
give thee, and then I must leave thee to defend
thyself.'

'Yet, tell me—' said Ered.

She came closer to him. Her eyes, fixed by
her thought, rested on his face. Her voice did not
tremble, though its tone was low.

'If it is true . . . if the gods need a sacrifice . . .

Oh, I could bear it from thy hands,' cried Ered.
· Thou wouldst be kind, and wouldst not be *glad*
to hurt me.   If it would save Ascar . . . I will
stand still, and be brave.   Even if I tremble I will
not cry.'

'*I*, Estra!' cried Olbri, and recoiled in horror.
' If it were to save Ascar's life I could not touch
thee.   No! live for Ascar.   And now listen for a
moment; for though I cannot stay with thee, I
will do for thee what I can.   Thou seest these
jewels?   They are all the wealth I have.   But I
need no wealth to accomplish *my* design.   Take
them.   Fasten them into thy hair, thy raiment.
They may ransom Ascar from his enemies.   And
then escape.   Thou art in utmost danger here,
from the Rema, from Ascar's servants, in danger
everywhere.   Escape at once.   Find thy way to
the Ekelfah ; thou wilt be safer in the desert than
in the Fair Country.   Listen once more.   Estri
Ascar is the prisoner of the Rema.   Take the
jewels with thee . . . I can only speak to thee for
a moment. . .   Wear thy slave's dress.   Keep thy
face closely veiled.   And, Estra—since thou hast
a gentle maiden's courage—I will say to thee,
"Wear a dagger, for thou art beautiful!"   Ah,
take the jewels!   They are of no use to me.
It is not with jewels that I shall meet the
sorcerer.'

He poured the jewels into her hands ; then

stood silent for a moment. 'And now, Estra, fare-well. I am sorry for thee. There was once a woman, as beautiful as thou art, who looked on me with a woman's pity. I have never forgotten her. Farewell, Estra, we must face our destinies. It is not likely that we shall meet again. Pray to thy gods to spare Ascar and thyself, and think kindly of me . . .'

As he took her hands, Ered murmured,—'We shall meet in the Spirit-land.'

Olbri looked down into her eyes, which were deep and steadfast, and in that instant of parting could not mock her for her faith. He said with a gentle accent, though he smiled,—

'And then we shall say: "We came here by different paths. But that need not trouble us, since we have met."'

He knelt down before her, and pressed his lips upon her hands. . . . And then he was gone, and she was alone in the courtyard. The faint stars looked down on her, shining from far away. She saw them, then covered her face with both her hands.

Thus they met for a few short instants, friend and bride, the companions of Ascar on his wed-ding-night. Let us leave them for a while to the darkness and the stars, and return to the Lord of the Escola.

VIII.

Whatever crazy sorrow saith,
No life that breathes with human breath
Has ever truly longed for death.

'Tis life, whereof our nerves are scant,
Oh life, not death, for which we pant;
More life, and fuller, that I want.

'THEY will come back,' said Ascar.

The sound of the horses' feet had died away; on all sides there was intense stillness. The quietness of the dawn was everywhere, over the blue, distant hills, the wide, unbroken plain. In the sky was the glow of the sunrise.

'They will come back,' said Ascar.

Why did Ascar repeat this sentence? What made him certain that the Rema would return? He did not know, but he had no doubt of the fact —he told himself that he would be a fool if he doubted it. There was no reason for him to wish for them; he was safer from suffering when he was alone. And yet an indefinite terror grasped his

VOL. I.   H

heart, and his eyes sought for some sign of his captors in the distance. There was no sign. But still they would return.

As he was certain that they would return, he was able to turn his mind to other thoughts. He looked at the barren, plain, the distant hillsides, at a silver thread of a river, observed for the first time. What river was this? Not the Tordrade, certainly. And not the river of Blue Waters, for—

Why should it not be the river of Blue Waters? He tried to think, but he found that he could not think. He tried to interest himself in the distant hills. These hills might be— To think was impossible.

The Rema had not given him any food that morning. He would share their provisions, no doubt, when they returned. As they had departed in the early morning they would be returning . . . at noon . . . The next words were more distinct.

'*The Rema often leave their prisoners to starve.*'

For one instant his heart stood still. And then every pulse began throbbing feverishly.

'Why'—cried the reaction—'should they have carried him so far? *They wished to take from you the least chance of escape.*'

But why—why? They had no reason for such cruelty. After all, they were men, though they had the name of fiends.

' *Ah,*' cried the mocking voice, ' *dost thou not yet believe in cruelty ?   To what purpose hast thou been the prisoner of the Rema ?* '

His heart sank.   Even if they intended to come back, they would not hasten because he was in need of food.   Many things might hinder them. And then, when at last they found him, he might be too weak—he would not think of their return. He would turn his mind away to another subject. This might be the River of Blue Waters after all.

No, he would not think of the River of Blue Waters.   Life and death were of more consequence than the Blue River.

Hunger ! What a horrible, slow suffering it was !   How long would it take to kill him ? He was still young, strong.   Oh, they meant him to suffer, they enjoyed his agony.   Then he would not suffer.   He would rise above the pain.   A man with a man's strength, has power to resolve.   He had resolved—and yet he was hungry.

Tears came into Ascar's eyes, and his exalted feelings vanished.   No, there was no advantage to be gained from unreal heights.   He would take other ground.   How many good men had suffered, and had suffered pain that was far worse than this.   A day or two of pain should be nothing to a man ; or, at any rate, a great experience.   He would try to feel gratitude for this new lesson—and then came the cry of the heart,—' If I could *live*.'

He felt stronger. The wish had relieved him. He would make an effort to be brave. The sun was rising, it would soon be mid-day. And then, with a start, he remembered unexpectedly that one of the Rema had spoken of 'mid-day.' It was all explained! They intended to return at noon. He had been a fool, overpowered by needless terror. Certainly they had not spoken of returning ; but then—' I will not doubt, because doubt is agony.' At any rate, there could be no possible harm in waiting quietly until noon had come.

Somewhat relieved, Ascar looked out on the morning, as lovely a morning as could speak peace to the heart of man ; for although a long, barren plain stretched in front of him, it was not desolate beneath the deep blue of the sky. In the distance, some clouds dyed the ground with purple shadows ; still further, the outlines of hills were bathed in light ; and, searching to discover objects in that light, he imagined he could discern shining mountain peaks. Everything was as beautiful in colour, and as peaceful, as if this were not a world in which men died miserably, as if there were no eyes willing to close to all the beauty, if only death would come to release them from suffering.

'Ered believes in the Akbare,' thought Ascar, lingering on the words as if they were a caress— 'but then, why do not the gods in the White Heaven send them to help us when we are in need of help?' Perhaps the gods *did* send them. Ascar did not know. He knew that his bonds were strong, there came no release from them.

So he waited through a weary morning, and his hunger became sharp, although he absorbed himself in many tasks, counting the clouds, imagining trees upon the hills, following the course of the river with his eyes. No effort could make him forget that he was hungry, but these tasks could occupy the surface of his mind. As the sun rose, however, all else was overwhelmed in the torture that can be caused by heat and light.

What could he do? He could not stir from the rock, could not even put up his hands to shield his face; the rock burned behind him, his eyelids appeared burned; he was bathed in torture, scorched in seas of fire. And then, as the blinding glare lessened with the motion of the sun, whilst still faint, giddy, and overwhelmed with heat, he was roused to consciousness by the agony of thirst which made the torture of hunger seem as nothing.

'Oh, cried Ascar, 'in future, whatever suffering I have, I will think it nothing if I have only water to drink!'

Oh! it was cruel! Why must he see the river,
the silver gleam of a river, not very far away; why
must he think perpetually of the stream below the
Escola where he and Olbri had bathed in summer
days? He could see the flecks of light falling
through the branches, could feel the water—the
cold water—close to him, at his lips, in his burning
throat. . . . He tore desperately at his chains. In
vain! there was no help in the solitude . . . the
noon had already come; he was alone. But there is
no need to repeat in every detail the endless history
of a day of agony.

The sun sank at last. Ascar watched it with
sad eyes. He had been weeping, but he was calm
now, though very tired. It seemed to him that he
looked into endless space, the *Silence of the gods*
which must even now be close. His life rose before him as if it were a phantom—Ered, Olbri, rose
with it, but they were phantoms too—and still
the sun sank in waves of gold and crimson, like
some great monarch who will not abate one jot of
his splendour because his subjects are starving.
He wished to pray, but he could not form sentences
. . . his head was faint, there were strange shadows
on the plain. . . . What was this? The tower of
the Escola was burning; dark figures dragged
away Ered . . . he could not move. . . . With a
start he awoke. Stars were shining in the sky;
the whole great plain was lost in a depth of night.

He tried to remember what had happened ; but he was too weak . . . he fell back to unconsciousness.

Voices were near him. He was lying on the ground, supported by a strong arm, leaning on a shoulder. He tried to raise his head, but he was too weak to stir. A voice spoke distinctly :

'You see he is alive.'

'What if he is ? '

'If he is,' cried the voice (the words came from the man who was supporting Ascar). 'If he is alive he is my prisoner, he belongs to me! I found him, and I will take care of him. Here! Here!'

With each word some cordial touched Ascar's lips. For a moment he raised his head, and then his eyes closed again.

'But you must not sleep,' exclaimed his possessor, shaking him. 'It is time to wake. The sun is ris- ing. Drink.'

Remembering his thirst, Ascar drank long and eagerly. The draught was bitter, but it seemed to be a stimulant. Suddenly he started. Where was the rock, where were his bonds? He would have fallen, but a hand caught him back again.

'Lay your head on my shoulder,' the voice said to him. 'Rest.'

The tone had the unmistakable accent of a friend. Stranger still, although Ascar was almost

too weak to wonder, it spoke in the language of
the Alidrah. But now the other voice uttered
sterner words, though also in some dialect of the
Fair Country.

'Thou art a fool, Ivlon,' said the other voice.
'What canst thou do with him now thou hast
released him? Dost thou think that we. shall be
able to take him with us over all the way between
us and Alvo's camp?'

Alvo! With a start Ascar realised that if he
had been released he was still a prisoner. The
name of the master-fiend recalled his senses. With
a stronger effort he raised his head once more.

'Ah! we will take him to the Leader,' Ivlon
cried. 'The Estri will understand what to do
with him. See! he is awake, he moves, he is alive.
Lean against the rock if thou wilt, man, and look
at us.'

Ascar did look. Faint, exhausted as he was,
he began to experience some return of consciousness.

The day had dawned. By its pale light he was
aware that he was seated on the ground, beneath
the rock, and that two men were in front of him,
looking at him curiously, their figures framed
by the vast extent of plain and sky. One of
these men was older than the other, not tall, but
with almost a giant's breadth and strength; the
other was young, with blue eyes, tangled curls,

and a frame slim with youth, but active and sinewy. Roughly armed were these men, but each had sword and shield, and a rude cap of steel upon his head ; each, too, had golden rings on wrists and ankles, a wallet on his shoulder, and a long knife in his belt. Who were these soldiers, and by what design or chance had they delivered him, and made him their prisoner? On their part they also seemed to be considering, as they stood before him, looking down on him.

'Your name,' demanded the elder, in a cold, impassive voice.

Ascar hesitated for an instant, then answered quietly.

' Of what country art thou ? '

' I come from the Alidrah.'

' How art thou here ? '

' I am a prisoner of the Rema.'

' There is no need to tell us,' Ivlon cried. ' No soldiers but the Rema let their prisoners starve.'

The other checked him by a movement of his hand.

' How long hast thou been bound here ? '

' Since yestermorn.'

Ivlon interrupted.

' He is a deserted prisoner. He belongs to us, Uldic, and we will take care of him.'

' Thou art always a fool. He is Maravel Ursan's prisoner.'

'What does that matter? Maravel Alvo shall decide.'

'It is even possible that he is an Estri. If he is an Estri we must leave him to his fate.'

'Art thou an Estri?' Ivlon asked of Ascar, looking down on him with eyes blue as the sky.

The nobleman hesitated, then assented by a sign.

Ivlon shook with laughter. 'He tells the truth.'

'But Uldic, I tell thee this business is not a jest. No leader may meddle with another's prisoner. Come on one side.'

And they conferred together; whilst Ascar, with a proud instinct, turned his face away. His *life* depended on the decision of these men, of whom one was a boy—was younger than himself . . . but then, life was a weary matter, and if they saved him from the rock, a *short* death. . . . The men came close to him again.

'Burden yourself with him,' Uldic said to his companion. 'But if the Rema ask for him you must give him up.' Observing the sauciness of his companion's face, he added, 'If you will not yield, the man must die.'

'I am not strong enough to fight thee!' Ivlon cried. Then, touching Ascar's shoulder, 'You are my prisoner, Estri.' An involuntary expression crossed the face of the nobleman. 'Better than starvation,' said Ivlon, drawing in his lips.

'Give me your knife, Uldic, that I may cut the

cords at his ankles. They are tight! The Rema are always kind to prisoners. And now, Estri, lean on me, and eat and drink. Not too much. Just enough to keep life in thee.'

'Thou wilt gain nothing by all this trouble,' Uldic said, whilst his companion fed Ascar as if he had been a child. 'Since he is an Estri we must take him to the Leader. And the Leader will not keep Ursan's prisoner.'

His tone was expressive, but Ascar pretended not to hear, whilst Ivlon touched his arm in assurance of protection. The nobleman felt the touch, but took no notice, for he had not yet decided how he ought to treat his owners. These soldiers of Alvo were his country's enemies—he must not seek favours from those his land had cursed—

'We must start,' said Uldic. 'The day will soon be hot.'

'My prisoner is tired. Go on. We will follow thee.'

'If thou wilt stay, I shall lie down by the rock and sleep.'

Uldic made the announcement with deep-toned dignity. He lay down forthwith in the shadow of the rock, and Ivlon stirred him impudently with his foot to show Ascar that he slept.

'Keep near him, Estri. I will sit and watch the sun.'

His eyes rested kindly upon his prisoner; but Ascar turned his head with conflicting feelings, and, leaning against the rock, closed his eyes, and feigned to sleep. He did not need to feign long, being faint, bewildered, scarcely able to realise that he had returned to life. Visions floated round him as he tried to thank the Akbare, but they were formless as phantoms in darkness—and he slept.

I X.

. . . That turneth the shadow of death into the
morning, and maketh the day dark with night.

THE sun was high when he awoke. A heavy
sleep had revived him; and, although he was still
tired, and stiff with fatigue and pain, he had
such a sensation of relief from intolerable oppression as he had never known since he had been
the prisoner of the Rema. The Rema were gone;
he was no longer fettered to the rock, his bond-
age was renewed under more favourable condi-
tions—he felt as if he were once more the Ascar
of old days who had entered the dark wood on
his wedding-night. Eagerly he covered his face
that he might thank the Akbare; and, addressing
himself to the Spirits of the sun and the winds,
he promised them that he would lead a better
life, so that he might face the silence more courage-
ously next time. What said the wise men?
'Give the poor of thy harvests; and speak not
as a friend with those thy land has cursed.' The

first of these virtues was out of his power at
present; but the last—

Turning his head, he saw that Ivlon was seated
on the ground, his knees clasped, his tangled
curls gleaming in the sunlight; and quick instincts
stirred him in favour of the bright-faced lad who
had treated him with so much generosity. But
then—why were the gods angry with himself, and
with his country? Was it not because of his
friendship, of his love? Should he now draw
fresh vengeance upon Ered, upon Olbri, by ill-
omened attraction to one of Alvo's men? With
natural gratitude, instinctive leanings, struggled
the new thoughts captivity had roused. Some
notion of duty had indeed awaked within him,
as yet strangely tangled, but still a reality.

Ivlon, for his part, looked towards his prisoner
as if more than ready for a bright conversation;
but, observing that the nobleman did not return
his glances, turned his head away, whilst his face
took graver lines. Yet when Uldic, awaking,
slowly stirred himself, he sprang up as quickly
as if he had been a child, and occupied himself
in preparations for a meal with what seemed
habitual lightheartedness. It was only when he
had spread his own portion on the ground that
he looked again towards the nobleman.

'Come and eat, Estri,' he said, in formal tones.

Without replying, Ascar rose and came to him.

They sat together. Ivlon divided in two parts his simple portion of black bread and vegetables ; and, yielding to his companion that which appeared the most attractive, occupied himself with the disposal of his own. Not a word said either, but, young creatures as they were, their meal disappeared without the aid of conversation ; and it was only when its conclusion compelled directer intercourse that the feeling of constraint became again intolerable. For Ivlon asked his companion if he were satisfied ; and Ascar, for answer, made a sign of assent.

'The Estri is too proud to speak to thee,' said Uldic.

Ivlon gave an impatient movement with his shoulders, and then laughed.

Ascar was stung ; and, as Uldic turned away, he made an earnest attempt to explain himself.

'Indeed, I am grateful,' he began ; but the young soldier interrupted.

'You would be grateful, Estri, if I were not one of Alvo's men. Keep your gratitude for your own countrymen.'

Ascar watched him uneasily as he moved to Uldic, but by degrees became lost in reflections of his own. Strange reflections ! stirring in the shadow of the rock, whilst the great plain stretched before him beneath the sky.

Where was Ered ? where Olbri ?—for since he

had been the captive of the Rema he had been
allowed little leisure in which even to think of
them.   When should he return his friend's familiar
greeting, or take up once more the broken wedding-
night ?   He could not imagine them in pain or
danger, perhaps he could not have borne such
agony ; he rather thought of them as waiting far
away, whilst he lay and looked at the sunlight on
the plain.   Ered ! with her eyes full of solitary
fancies, her dreams of communion with gods and
spirits !—when should he take his dreamer in his
arms, and kiss her from visions into womanhood ?
Olbri scarcely believed in the gods . . . but his remembrance of his bride brought always with it a
link with the Unseen.   And yet it was not only of
the Unseen he thought as he lay and dreamed
of a marriage-festival.

He might have been occupied with more serious
meditation after a day in the valley of the
shadows ; but, once delivered from the rock and
from the Rema, his released thoughts sprang back
to old desires.   To do him justice, in the background of his heart another feeling was also
powerful.

'I have seen the face of the Silence,' Ascar
thought.   'Next time we meet it will be familiar.'

He lay and pondered ; and, at a little distance,
Ivlon and Uldic were busy with their plans, unconscious that, hidden in a rocky cleft, there

looked down on them an unthought-of auditor.
For there lay a little Rema, a small, dark, grinning
creature, his ears quivering with a true spy's eagerness, his lips parted as if with utmost delight he
were drinking in all the two companions said.
Satisfied at last, he stretched himself a little—for
he had been concealed in the cleft a day and
night—snapped his fingers noiselessly to signify
contempt, and stirred with a quick, noiseless
motion from his place. Keeping the rock between
himself and the three men, he clambered lightly
down the other side of it; and with one or two
backward glances to be sure that it concealed
him, ran with swift, bare feet across the plain.
Let us follow in the track of this ominous circumstance and learn the meaning of the espial,
while the three companions remain beneath the
rock, unconscious that danger may be near them.
Alas! even when the shadow of death has been
turned into the morning, it is still possible for the
day to become dark with night.

Danger was near. To the north, not far away,
the plain was broken by a hollow and a tree; and
there, somewhat sheltered from the intense glare
of the sun, was gathered the band of Rema. Iscar
was there, leaning against the tree; and Corlon,
and Corlon's men, squatted on the ground; and a
few horses, tethered to some stakes; and the spy,
relating his story. His words were received with

breathless interest, but also, it seemed, with some perplexity.

'The men are waiting for the Effar,' said the spy.

'The Effar have departed,' answered Corlon, grinning.

'To the north,' added Iscar, and then all were silent, and the spy squatted on the ground amongst the rest.

They all appeared to be pondering ; even Iscar, whose face alone preserved its impassiveness. As he leaned against the tree he was a conspicuous figure, and it may not be out of place to speak of him. For he was one of the most distinguished leaders who belonged to the camp of the old Maravel.

Iscar was young, but had been a soldier all his life. Although a Rema, he was tall, slender, supple, with regular features, an expression curiously impassive, and a figure which promised much agility. He had the reputation, singular in Ursan's camp, of being cold, without ambition, even indifferent to plunder ; and this in spite of the favour openly shown to him by Ursan, who always valued a leader of intelligence. And yet there were such stories told of Iscar's youth, tales of wild courage and generosity, as could not be whispered of any other leader, with the exception of Alvo, who was beyond all competition. No

doubt it was the success of that brilliant rival
which inspired the Rema leader to a different
career ; and, indeed, his unvarying austerity con-
trasted with the caprices of Ursan's favourite.
Severe, pitiless, haughty even to his master, Iscar
was not popular amongst the leaders, though his
attention to every form of duty met continual
recompense from the old Maravel. Ursan, who
passed a keen judgment on his leaders, had whispered these words to Rudol, his confidant,—

'Iscar is clever, and as hard as iron, but he will
never govern men as Alvo does.'

Few envied Iscar; the jealousy of Rema leaders
had long been directed to another favourite.

And now—that favourite was in the minds of
all as the little band lay in the hollow, beneath
the tree ; for the thought of the young leader
could not be far away from those who had just
heard news of 'Alvo's men.' It is possible, therefore, that the words they spoke may serve as some
clue to events already shadowed — linking the
story of our captive Estri to that of the enemy
most feared by the Alidrah. For a while there
was silence, as if no one dared to speak ; but at
length Corlon could restrain himself no longer.

'Ar-r,' muttered Corlon, 'I wish it were their
master.'

From his erect position Iscar looked down
quietly.

'You have reason for the wish,' he said, with a tone quiet as his face, 'since Alvo always strikes at the leader.'

Corlon started angrily, and with an impatient movement almost drew the long knife which he carried in his belt.

'Alvo!' he cried, 'he is surrounded by his Exiles, who would die rather than let his finger ache! If he were alone— But Iscar cares for Alvo, although Alvo takes Iscar's place in the Leopard's camp. Iscar loves Alvo so much—'

'So much,' echoed Iscar, quietly, 'that if I were aiming at his heart my hand would not tremble. But he saved my life.'

From his manner of utterance he appeared to be making a confession on which he had previously determined.

Corlon looked up in amazement, and an expression of spiteful triumph began to gather in his narrow Rema eyes.

'Ah! ah!' he cried, 'I think I know the tale. Iscar was in danger, and cried out to the young leader—'

Iscar interrupted him, still speaking quietly, but with the tone of one who has made up his mind to speak. The men who lay in the shadow of the branches looked up towards him with unusual interest.

'A likely tale!' he said. 'Iscar does not call

for help from Alvo. But he gave it, unasked—and
till I have paid him wound for wound— Listen!
you may hear the story once for all. You had
better listen, for I shall not speak of it again.'

He paused, for a slight wind had stirred amongst
the leaves, and on that hot day a breeze was of
consequence. When he went on speaking, however, it was in the same pausing manner, as if he
were almost indifferent to his words. But the
Rema were listening with too much interest to be
affected by his impassiveness.

'We were returning from an expedition against
the Nira,' Iscar said—'and Corlon was with us,
although he has forgotten—and Alvo, Rudol were
there—and the Nira came on us suddenly, attack-
ing us before we could gain the camp. I had hurt
my foot, and could not keep up with the rest, and
there was not a Rema who chose to stay with me
—Rudol was anxious to be with his Maravel—and
Corlon was far in front—seeking glory—'

Corlon started, and uttered a sudden curse;
but Iscar only waited till his companion was
silent. His cold voice suited ill with his narrative,
but it might have concealed more feeling than it
showed.

'Alvo was with us—he was as mad as usual,
and had chosen to wear no armour, and no weapon
but his sword. But he came to me when he saw
I was left alone, and fought, as Alvo fights.'

'Ar-r,' cried Corlon, sinking down, 'he can turn those thin wrists so that none can see them move. May all the wood-devils curse his insolence! He knows the trick of it. I wish I did too!'

Iscar continued, without heeding him,—

'Ursan must have been anxious—lest his favourite should be killed. He sent men to our relief, and they came to us—when I was struck to my knees, and Alvo's eyes were full of blood.'

Again Corlon interrupted,—

'Then it was upon that day the young leader gained the scar which spoiled his woman's beauty!'

And again Iscar continued, as if he had not heard,—

'Ursan came to see his son's wounds—he was not interested in mine!'

'Ursan is fond of his son,' Corlon said in explanation, for Iscar's impassive voice had at last shown some emotion. 'And it is a rare sight to see Alvo when his wounds are being dressed! I have heard him cry out, though he almost died of shame. That is your brave man!'

'He is brave,' said Iscar, quietly. 'I hate him, but no man shall speak ill of him to me. He took my hands the next day before the camp; he knew I could not draw back, and I hated him the more. But he has been wounded for me, and I must pay him wound for wound. When I have paid him—' he paused—'I will speak with him.'

'Ha! ha!' laughed Corlon. 'We all hate the young leader.' He lay on his back, looking through the leaves to the blue sky. 'Is it not so, Nardi?'

'Truly,' answered the spy, with emphasis.

'And why dost *thou* hate him?'

'Because he is one of Ursan's leaders.'

Corlon wriggled.

'And thou—dost thou hate the young leader, Lipsus?'

Lipsus was a Rema who had joined the band that day. He raised to his leader a shrewd, simple face, resting on a mighty hatchet, which he clasped with both his arms.

'I have never seen him.'

'Wouldst thou be afraid to strike him?'

'I would follow the Maravel,' said Lipsus, with an innocent expression.

Some of the men laughed, and Corlon frowned angrily. Again there was silence, whilst a hot wind stirred the leaves.

'The young leader has a pretty face,' Nardi muttered with disdain.

'He is brave, notwithstanding,' cried Corlon, who never held to his own statements. 'And he can talk any language as if it were his own. But he belongs to the Alidrah, and shall be cursed by all of us.'

'Except Maravel Ursan,' Nardi muttered, spitefully.

'Except Ursan,' echoed Iscar, with a quiet intonation.

'And these are his men,' said Nardi.

The words were received in silence. Possibly they suggested fancies which could not be easily expressed. The heat of the day had come, and the men lay down and slept, pressed together in little space beneath the branches of the tree.

Meanwhile (to return to our captive nobleman) Estri Ascar and his guardian had spent a pleasant morning, for it had been decided that Uldic should search for the missing Effar, whilst Ivlon kept watch over the prisoner. The young men were not displeased with this arrangement; for, although their intercourse was constrained, their youth drew them to each other, and in the absence of Uldic they could act with greater freedom. With few words, they went down together to the river; and bathed, and then rested together on the bank, looking at each other now and then with laughing eyes, and then turning their faces away more solemnly. The day was glorious, the sun blazed in the sky, the great plain appeared to be one flood of light—and Ascar could not but remember the delirium, the thirst, the agony of death through which he had passed yesterday. Was he indeed delivered from the Silence, and what would be the lot of his recovered life? Ah!

was not the Fair Country somewhere in the distance . . . where friend and bride waited for him?

In the greatest heat of the day they left the river, returned to the rock, and lay down in its shade—Ivlon rubbing his eyes to keep himself awake, and Ascar lying with closed eyes, but not asleep. He had been supplied with garments from the store of his young guardian, for his own were ragged, and in some places stiff with blood; and the delicious comfort occasioned by the change was only embittered by the difficulty of gratitude. For whenever he opened his lips the young soldier turned away his head—proving in this manner that he had his share of pride. No matter! it was certain at any rate that he was kind—and Ascar lay in the shadow, and left perplexities alone. It was pleasant to lie still, and dream .·. . and sleep sometimes . . . beneath the great rock which had been the rock of agony.

'There is Uldic,' cried Ivlon, starting up to meet his comrade, and then looking down on the nobleman with a ludicrous expression; for the instinct which prompted him to rush to his companion was being restrained by his sense of guardianship. Mindful of new dignity, he kept his post, whilst Uldic came with slow steps across the plain — so slowly that his walk had an expression of ill-humour, which, as soon as he reached them, became evident in words.

'This is your fault, Walna.'

'Everything always is my fault.'

'This is your fault,' Uldic repeated steadily.

It appeared that the Effar could not be found, or the horses they had promised, and that it was not possible to wait for them any longer.

Uldic ascribed this difficulty to the delay which had been occasioned by the release of the prisoner.

'We should not be here at all if it had not been for thy folly.'

By this and similar reproaches, Ascar learned that the soldiers had been forbidden to venture near the Rema, but that the younger had attempted an excursion by himself. It seemed that Uldic had some reason for the displeasure which he expressed in few words, but severely.

'I will tell Estri Alvo.'

'And he will be angry,' Ivlon cried, with an imperfect attempt to seemed alarmed. He added, throwing up his hands with a childish gesture. 'Ah! how many times I have been summoned to his tent! He is always so good to me, our little Estri! I must begin to be better.'

'Thou art always beginning,' Uldic said. And Ivlon:—

'When I see Estri Alvo next I will begin.'

With that they began their journey across the plain, the journey that was to take them to the young leader's camp. Ascar looked back once at the rock as they moved away.

Was danger nearer? The hollow which had a tree was no longer crowded with the forms of Rema soldiers; one only was left, seated upon the roots, with his chin on the enormous hatchet which he clasped in both his arms. Deserted by the rest, and forbidden to leave his post, Lipsus was fulfiling the duty of sentinel, a hated office, which he owed on this occasion to his suggestive answer to Maravel Corlon's question. He sat there, desolate, like a carved wood-demon, hugging his beloved hatchet as if that could give him consolation. A sudden footstep! he started to his feet, and became aware of the approach of Maravel Iscar.

'Go after the others, Lipsus.'

'Maravel, I am a sentinel.'

'Do not answer me, fool. Go after the others. I will remain here, and join the next band of Rema. Hast thou no ears, fool? Go after Corlon's men.'

For one instant Lipsus lingered, looking doubtful, but the command of Maravel Iscar was not to be disputed; and, moreover, it dawned triumphantly upon him that his hatchet and himself would now be in the fight. He threw up his arms with a shrill cry of delight, and then fled away with the utmost rapidity; whilst Iscar, quietly assuming his position, looked out in his turn over the wide extent

of plain.   Had he not done well? there was not
another leader who would have taken the office of
sentinel.   Seated beneath the tree, with a face
watchful and intent, although not a feature moved,
he looked out across the plain.

What was to happen to these men, Alvo's men?
What could be the meaning of the old Maravel
—of this device which, take what course it would,
could hardly be fulfilled without some expenditure
of blood?   He would not be present to see Alvo's
men ill-treated, although he did not love the men
better than their master—his bond held him, for he
was resolutely determined that he would do his
duty to his gratitude.   So pondered Iscar, seated
beneath the tree and looking out upon the sunlit
plain.   He gave himself credit for his resolution,
for it is not always an easy duty—gratitude.

Was the captive Estri grateful?—himself reclining at that instant with his two companions beneath
the shelter of a tree, one of the rare trees which
could be found here and there, to the relief of
travellers over the Ekelfah.   His strength had
given way during the long, weary march, and
Ivlon had insisted that he himself was tired, so
they had all lain down beneath the shelter of the
branches to allow themselves a few moments' rest
or sleep.   They had travelled far.   The Essil was
lost in the distance, but the great plain still lay

around them on every side, flooded with sunlight
although the sun was sinking, and apparently
empty of all travellers but themselves. Ivlon lay
on his face, with his head resting on his hands, and
the sun shining through his tangled curls. And
Ascar, looking out over the great plain, found his
survey arrested by the sight—and by bitterness.

Was it not natural? He was tired, exhausted,
bent with the weight of unspeakable depression ; a
captive before whom hung a doubtful fate, who
was, perhaps, being dragged over the weary plain
to die. And, meanwhile, this lad — this boy,
younger than himself — the spoiled, wilful favourite, as it seemed, of a camp and a camp's
master, was bright with hope, with health, with
the power of bestowing favours, was without knowledge of the trials of prisoners. If *he* had been
torn from his country and his home, not even permitted to complete his wedding-night, why, then,
even *he*, so ready to be kind, might find it difficult
to be generous. Ascar would be grateful ; he intended to be grateful, at the first opportunity he
would repay all benefits, but, meanwhile, an Estri of
the Alidrah must not speak freely with one of Alvo's
men. It was at this instant that Ivlon turned on
his side, and, raising his sword to his lips, pressed
kisses on it. The action was childish, and Ascar,
who observed it, did not find it difficult to be
contemptuous.

'The Estri scorns thee,' said Uldic, quietly; and then, as Ivlon started with rage, he slowly added; The Estri had no love for his own sword? No doubt it is in the hands of the Rema since he was their prisoner.'

Ascar turned pale, and bent his glance on the ground. The insult had wounded him too deeply for reply. Ivlon drew closer, his momentary anger checked by vexation deeper than his own.

'You think me a fool, Estri, because I kiss my sword? Well, you are right, but then you do not know. This is Alvo's sword. He has worn it. I will tell you—'

He seemed anxious that the prisoner should recover his composure. At the same time it was impossible not to hear the love and pride which rose with his voice when he pronounced his master's name. To Ascar that name was still almost fabulous, and he listened with strange thrills of bewilderment.

'I will tell you,' Ivlon repeated. 'A band of Effar went out to plunder. I asked to be sent with them, and they were angry; and when we came back at night they refused me any spoil. They said I was not of their band, although I had fought with them. But Alvo came out to give away the spoil, and he was wearing for the first time his beautiful, new sword. And he would take no notice how the plunder was divided, but kept on giving it till there was nothing left. And then, when my turn came and there was no share left for me, he took his sword out of its sheath and gave it to me. Alvo's sword!' cried Ivlon, pressing the hilt against his breast.

And Ascar thought,—

'The wizard knows how to win the hearts of men.'

'Look, Estri!' cried Ivlon, with still greater friendliness. 'Here is the inscription, "Akbare, help me and my sword;" and here is the leader's name, "Alvo;" and mine, "Walna of the Ivloni." Alvo says the good spirits will not help us if the sword is ever lost.'

'What good spirits are these?' thought the nobleman, who was not an exile. 'Not the Akbare of the Fair Country.'

(So much remained of an Estri's education to the friend of a sorcerer and husband of a slave.)

'We must start,' said Uldic, heaving up his great frame slowly.

They all rose with lingering movements and murmurs of regret; for the shade had been pleasant, the sight of the green leaves, the interval of rest in the hot, weary march. Their rest was over, perchance more completely passed than any member of the little band imagined. As they turned their faces once more towards the plain there lay before them—a new experience.

The sun was sinking when at last they reached
some hills. They had travelled far, but they were
all in cheerful spirits, even Ascar, on whose account
the march was slow, for he was stronger now the
heat of the day was over. They had entered a
dark pass which shut out the glowing sky, and his
thoughts, dreamy from fatigue, were with his bride,
when, suddenly, his heart beat in long, heavy
throbs, and he stood still, overcome by agony.
Before him there was a band of dark-faced Rema,
like the men who had left him at sunrise the day
before. Ascar placed his hand on his eyes. For
one instant he imagined that this was a dream and
would pass away.

But his companions saw also.

'There are some Rema,' Ivlon cried, with the
pleased surprise of one ready for company.

Uldic looked grave. His eyes were on the band,
and he understood the meaning of their attitude.
All were still. On each side the hills rose like
precipices, and between their dark outlines the strip
of sky was red. And now Corlon stepped forward,
and Ascar saw and knew him. The horror of that
remembrance stopped his breath.

'Who are you?' asked Corlon.

'We belong to the young leader.'

'Who is that with you?'

'He is our prisoner.'

'You lie. He is ours.'

'Draw your swords,' cried Ivlon, gaily, 'and he shall belong to that man of us who is best.'

'You talk like a fool,' whispered Uldic in his ear. 'There are twenty men. You must leave this dispute to me.'

'Brothers,' he said in slow, impassive tones, 'our master is the son of your master. We must not dispute. Let me confer with you.'

He advanced a step—his foot caught in the bough of a crawling bush, and he fell. In an instant the Rema seized him; and then rushed to Ivlon, whose sword flashed out as he set his back against the rock. Ascar was unnoticed, might even have escaped, but he could not desert the men who had saved his life.

All unarmed as he was, he thrust himself among the Rema, who for one instant actually gave way. Before he had reached Ivlon, however, he was surrounded and dragged back, thrown over, and held with a sword against his throat. Ivlon maintained his position, motionless — his sword drawn, his young face white and set; and the Rema, seeing that he was desperate, hesitated to attack him. Then suddenly a little figure darted forward from one side, and struck a tremendous blow with a great hatchet—the shield of Ivlon turned it, but his shoulder was wounded; and the Rema, seeing his blood flow, were encouraged. They rushed on him; in an instant he was struck

down. . . . Ascar heard him fall, and his own heart
and strength gave way. He closed his eyes, and
waves seemed to close above him ; there followed
a few instants of unconsciousness.

He raised himself at last. His eyes were still
bewildered, but he was aware that he was no longer
held. The Rema stood about him in the dark
pass . . . his glance sought anxiously for his late
companions. He saw them at a little distance ;
they were both bound hand and foot ; they were
seated on the ground, with a guard of Rema near
them. On the face of the younger was restless
misery, but Uldic appeared resigned and indifferent.

'Uldic, speak to them. They do not understand.
Tell them about the prisoner.'

'It would do no good.'

'Tell them we are Alvo's men.'

'They know it well enough.'

'If I could have wounded one of them,' Ivlon
muttered, but Uldic only turned impatiently away.

Ascar looked at them both with a pity keen as
shame. What would be the fate of these men who
had saved his life? He could see how Ivlon's
restlessness chafed the skin upon his wrists, while
blood dripped slowly from his shoulder to the
ground.

'Come and be bound, old friend,' cried one of
the Rema. 'And tell your comrades our ways, for
you understand them.'

'Wait an instant,' said Ascar. He tore a strip off his sleeve, and bound the wound of Ivlon, clumsily enough. The young prisoner seemed too much bewildered to take notice of the action. Himself bound, Ascar sat down by the side of his companions.

What would happen next? What would be the end of this, not for himself but for the men who had saved his life? He could give them no comfort . . . he could not help them or himself . . . and the Gods in the White Heaven took no heed of prisoners. Ah! *he* knew what it was to be the captive of the Rema—but these men who had saved him, had been generous to him. . . .

'We are going to the land of the Rema,' said one of the soldiers.

The sun had set; the hills looked dark and wan; they set out on their march to the enemy's country.

X.

We will grieve not, rather find
Strength in what remains behind ;
In the primal sympathy
Which having been, must ever be,
In the soothing thoughts that spring
Out of human suffering.

So it must be; so it has ever been. But the
primal sympathy is not always on the surface.
The stars of heaven looked down on the three
captives, but the stars did not see them turn to
wards each other.

They went on through the night, travelling northwards amongst the hills. Their hands and feet
were bound, but it was possible to move. The
march led them down rough paths, round corners
of massive rocks ; and then upwards again, clamber-
ing and stumbling, whilst stars shone above their
heads. The shadows of hills were everywhere, but
here and there some edge of rock would glisten in
the moonlight ; though darkness slept in unfathomable crevices, or cast round them strange forms, as if

the rocks themselves were enchanted.   Once, turning
a corner, they could see below them the silver spray
of a waterfall; once a river shone in front of
them—the River of Blue Waters, said the Rema—
several times they passed bubbling springs, whose
sound was pleasant in the darkness.   Or there were
defiles, haunted by hosts of shadowy enemies; or
silver plains shining like water in the moonlight;
or great hills whose outlines were black against the
sky.   The march was a dream, but the night and
loneliness were dismal, and Ascar was glad when
the sky became pale with dawn.   The Rema shared
their horses, and walked and rode by turns, but for
the prisoners there was no relaxing of fatigue.
Ascar envied Ivlon's light footstep, and even Uldic's
heavy stride; his companions did not become weary
like himself.

So dawn came, and the sun—and the sun brought
the heat, and it soon became natural to wish for
night.   And Ascar flagged more and more, although
often reminded to be active by the sting of some
Rema's whip.

'Lean on me,' whispered Ivlon, without looking
at his companion.

It was the first word he had spoken to him since
they shared captivity.

Ascar paid no heed; but he had heard the little
sentence, and it conveyed to him some sense of
fellowship.   He could not but notice besides that

Ivlon slackened his own pace, though that slacken-
ing brought on him also showers of blows. The
Estri was grateful, but in the presence of the Rema
the expression of gratitude was impossible.

After all, there were pleasures—some intervals
of rest, whilst the Rema indulged themselves in
coarse jests or sleep; and Uldic stretched himself
out like a great log; and Ivlon crouched on the
ground, writhing miserably. To the Estri, worn
out by previous experiences, rest seemed like the
Heaven of the Gods itself; and he almost wondered
that his companion could have strength enough
left to be humiliated. Alas! he was right; a captive's many troubles do not long leave room for the
sense of degradation.

Not even to Ivlon. Through the second night,
Ascar, too tired to sleep, heard him toss and moan ;
but in the morning, whilst the soldiers were pre-
paring for their march, he sank down on the ground,
and slept as soundly as a child. Roughly roused,
he sprang up, surprised that he had slept, and his
light laugh rang out as it had done of old ; whilst
the two other captives, less inclined for mirth,
looked round on him with visible disgust. They
would have been wiser if they had not vexed themselves, for evidently laughter could not long be
possible. As the long days passed, and the weary
march went on, the captives seemed far enough removed from mirth.

'There is the Wall of Stone,' said Uldic suddenly one morning, gazing on a shadowy mass against the sky. He added, apparently seized by a sudden thought, 'They must be taking us to the Leopard's Den.'

'Then Ursan must know,' whispered Ivlon, who was startled.

Uldic made no answer, and they went on silently. But from that moment a deeper gloom took possession of Alvo's men—their captivity was more serious than they had thought.

On the next morning the Wall of Stone was climbed, no easy matter to those whose feet were bound. But the top was reached at last ; and they all lay down to rest, and gazed on the vast panorama on all sides—rocks, hillsides, mountains ; to the south the great Ekelfah, stretching far away to the invisible Fair Country. The sinking sun dyed the plain and rocks with crimson. Ascar lay and gazed with his whole heart in his eyes. Somewhere in the invisible distance lay his home, but the land of the Rema was nearer now . . . and death.

'Hola, Estri,' cried a Rema, 'art thou looking for the Alidrah? Shall I tell thee what is happening to thy pretty wife?'

The nobleman tried not to listen, but the first few words he heard brought the shudder of a pang which was worse than the fear of death.

'Thou art married then?' whispered a murmur

at his car, and he became aware that Ivlon lay at his side.

He gave a sign of assent, but could not speak ; at that moment he was in no mood for sympathy. No leisure was allowed for combat with the phantoms. They descended the Wall of Stone that night.

And then—through some long, slow days they again marched over a plain ; sombre, thirsty days of the most intense monotony. One scene, however, occurred which was distinct, which impressed itself on the prisoners' memory.

It was this. They had been travelling during a gloomy afternoon through a dense mist which obscured the earth and sky, with wet drops clinging to their garments and hair, until all, even the horses, were dejected. At night - fall they came to a hovel, the first human dwelling-place which the Estri had seen since his captivity began — built beneath a rock, with three trees in front of it, which flung out their arms on the mist like angry giants. From the door of the hovel a tall man came to receive them ; behind him was a gaunt woman, probably his wife.

So you have come again,' he said, in the language of the Rema.

' Ar-r,' asserted Corlon, with the Rema snarl.

· You have prisoners. Are they noblemen of the Alidrah ?'

' This one is an Estri.'

The man laughed unpleasantly, and pointed at his wife, twisting his thumb beneath his arm.

'*She* does not love the Estria.'

'No,' said the woman, 'I do not love them. I am one of the Sena. They have almost killed out my tribe. They are all devils. Are you taking this devil to the Leopard? I trust that Ursan will tear him limb from limb.'

Corlon looked disgusted, but the soldiers laughed The prisoners were turned into a dark shed, secured, and left. They were hungry and thirsty, but food and drink were scarce; and they were thankful to be allowed to rest. The shed, however, though damp, was intolerably hot; and fever and thirst made sleep impossible. The long night passed slowly; and they were watching the first light through the chinks when they heard the sound of a footstep outside the door. It was the woman who entered; and by the dim light of the dawn they could see that she bore a large jar upon her head.

She stooped to Uldic, and set the jar against his mouth; at the sound of his heavy draughts the others raised themselves enviously. Ascar lifted his dry lips as she raised the jar again; but she passed him, and went to the other side of the shed. He followed her with his thirsty, burning glance; and at that instant his eyes and Ivlon's met.

'Prisoners share alike,' said Ivlon to the woman.

She answered,—

'I give no water to an Estri of the Alidrah.'

'Still we will share,' he said, and buried his face in his arms; and seeing him resolute, she turned away; then, woman-like, returned after she had passed the entrance, and held out the jar to each, to Ascar first. Afterwards she occupied herself with offices for all, bathing their faces and feet, and pitying the marks of stripes; although, because of the scene described, or his good looks, or his youth, the youngest absorbed the largest share of her attention.

'I must go,' she said, as the pale light became stronger. 'He will find out afterwards, but I must be near him when he wakes.'

'Will he be angry?' Ivlon asked, and she laughed harshly, swung the jar on her shoulder, and went out through the entrance; leaving them to wonder till the sound of Rema voices warned them that the day's march would soon begin.

They were dragged from the shed, and came out with blinking eyelids, scarcely able at first to see the difference of the prospect; for the mist had cleared, a mountain rose above the hovel, and in the distance were white peaks, faint in morning light. The tall man stood talking to Corlon; in the shadow of the entrance there was the figure of the woman, motionless.

'Why, no!' cried a Rema, 'the great jar is

nearly empty; the prisoners must have been drinking.'

The owner gave a sudden start. He looked back at the woman, who advanced a pace, with a pale face, but with her head held scornfully.

'They have been drinking,' she said in a harsh voice.

He did not answer, but laid his hand upon her shoulder. Corlon, whose orders had been disobeyed, was furious; and called at once to one of the chief men of his band,—

'Take that woman, and scourge her.'

'There is no need,' said the man, standing quietly with his hand upon her shoulder.

She did not move, but she looked up into his face, and it was evident that she was afraid. The aspect of the man was so grim that Corlon took no further trouble, but began to arrange the details of the march.

In the confusion of the start it chanced that for one instant the woman was standing near the prisoners.

'I could not help it,' she said in a trembling whisper. 'They told me you were all to die. Some day he will kill me, and there will be an end of it.'

She shrank back as the Rema came between them, and they saw her no more.

As they travelled onwards, the eyes of Ascar and

Ivlon turned often back to look at the lonely
hovel, but soon it was only a black mark on the
mountain; and then a hillside came between and
it was lost. They had left it behind them like
the Wall of Stone, like the great Ekelfah, like the
Fair Country. And yet in the breasts of both the
young captives struggled the memory of that
lonely home.

That lonely home, that gaunt, careworn woman
—were there many such places in the corners of
the world?

Where were the gods, thought Ascar, who
should send down light from heaven, and give aid
to the feeble, and to prisoners? Would they protect Olbri, who had lost his friend; or Ered . . .?
The world was full of misery. And yet there were
still a few hands to help sufferers, and thirsty lips
that could turn away from water. Why could he
not speak to Ivlon? Ah! he had rejected him, he
had shown him an Estri's pride, and dared not
turn towards him now. And, meanwhile, through
Ivlon's young heart one sentence fluttered—the
words of the woman—'They told me you were all
to die.'

It was a new thought from which he could not
free himself, which closed round him like the mists
of yesterday; and yet, though he was conscious
that darkness was before him, he shrank like a
coward from contemplating it. Sometimes he

looked with piteous eyes at Uldic, but in Uldic's impassive face there was no encouragement. And still they went on, stumbling through wild mountain-districts, with a strange mountain-title—'Lumber-Rooms of God.' One more barren plain, one only, lay before them, and then the land of the Rema—and the end.

It was after they reached that last plain that their worst trials began.

One evening, when all were resting on the ground, they were roused by the unexpected appearance of two men. These were Nardi, who with Lipsus had been absent during the march; and another, who had not the appearance of a Rema. Any change was welcome, and the Rema roused themselves, whilst Corlon asked anxiously what news there was.

'Maravel Rudol comes.'

'Aha!' said Corlon.

'They say that he will take charge of the prisoners.'

'He may do so. Since he claims to be Ursan's favourite, he will be more shielded than I am from Maravel Alvo's wrath. Didst thou know Alvo?'

He turned to the visitor, a brown, fat specimen of a mountain-tribe.

'Ah! I knew him.'

' What didst thou think of him ? '

' I thought him a Noridah' *(handsome fellow) ;*
' he gave me a sword-belt.'

' But thou hatedst him ? '

' Ah ! '

Not another word was said, but the small, fat
visitor crossed to the prisoners. As he looked
down on Uldic, the captives saw that his lips
moved ; their murmur was almost inaudible :

' Your master's men should not be here.'

Then he turned away without a change of countenance ; and the captives also dared not express
their wonder. But to their friendless condition
there was untold value in a single word of
sympathy.

The next morning, when they had slept, and
were all about to start, Uldic found occasion to
whisper words to Ivlon ; for his experience, older
than that of his companion, foresaw that there
would be trouble when Maravel Rudol came. The
great Uldic, who bore all trials stolidly, had little
pity for his companion's impatience ; and as on
this occasion he deigned to give him warning he
was evidently afraid that the danger would be
grave. He was still speaking when the last night's
visitor came and stood in front as if he were sur-
veying him.

' Alvo's man ! ' he said, and his hands touched
Uldic's arm.

The Rema who were near him laughed uproari-
ously.

'Alvo's man!' he said again, as he paused in
front of Ivlon, gazing at him with what seemed
keener interest.

The Rema began telling him that 'the young
cub had hot blood, and Maravel Rudol—Maravel
Rudol would make it flow!'

Still the fat man gazed, and kept on touching
with his hand the cords which bound Ivlon, as if
unconsciously.

'Tell this to Alvo,' he whispered suddenly; and
then turned away, and was not seen by them
again.

With a cautious movement Ivlon slowly raised
his wrists. The cords which bound them had
been cut in several places. Ascar and Uldic saw,
and in an instant closed upon him to shield him
from detection by the Rema. Ivlon looked at
them with blue eyes that danced with joy. .

'It shall be for all of us, for all of us,' he said.

'Wait, wait,' muttered Uldic; 'we must choose
a fitting moment. Meanwhile, be patient, if thou
hast to wait for days.'

They stood together. Ascar looked across the
plain to some peaks in the distance, dark against
a yellow sky. He wondered that he could not
hope—perhaps because he had been so long a
captive—for surely some hope was now permis-

sible. All at once there rose before his eyes the
dark wood, and the torches, the dead bodies of
his companions; and, as he started at the vision,
he saw what had caused it, for near him was the
face of Rudol, as he had seen it on his wedding-
night. A mean face, gazing at him with a cruel
smile—oh! had not fresh danger arrived with the
Maravel?

In a few more instants the little band divided,
and rough steeds bore away Corlon and his men,
whilst the grating voice of Rudol could be heard
giving directions, which the Rema on all sides
obeyed abjectly. The march began. The captives were placed in the centre, with enemies sur-
rounding them on every side — a circumstance
which caused Ivlon to assume great demureness,
although now and then he tossed his yellow curls.
Beneath enforced caution his young face gleamed
with hope, though its outlines were sunken by
captivity. He felt the responsibility of his position; he must be cautious, must not be impatient.

'Nardi,' cried a Rema, 'what hast thou done
with thy new sword?'

'I gave it to the Maravel,' said Nardi, screwing
his mouth into a smile.

'Thy new sword?'

'Ah! It has Alvo's name upon it. I knew
Maravel Rudol would love one of Alvo's swords.
Look at the eyes of the young one,' for Ivlon

had turned round anxiously. 'Here is Maravel Rudol to answer for himself.'

Rudol came up, swaggering, with his new sword at his side, and at once kicked the youngest prisoner, and commanded him to walk faster. Then, when Ivlon obeyed, he struck him with his whip, and told him to walk slower; he would teach him how to walk! Without mounting his horse, he paced onwards by the prisoners, eyeing them to discover some excuse for punishment. It was upon Ivlon that his mind was chiefly fixed—on Ivlon, whose colour came and went so easily!

'So! we have heard from Alvo,' he announced in a loud voice, gratified because the news made Ivlon start. 'He will do nothing for these men, his Exiles. Alvo has no spirit with which to help his men.'

'It is false,' cried Ivlon.

Rudol looked at him with a smile.

'So thou canst believe in thy master? The Rema know him better. This is how thy master writhes when his wounds are being dressed.' He made some clumsy movements, and the Rema laughed.

'Maravel,' said Ivlon, in a humble voice, 'I must entreat thee not to speak against my master.'

Rudol's eyes shone, and with a motion of his fingers he demanded attention from every member

of the band. A moment of triumph! in which,
by one crowning insult, he could inflict shame on
Alvo as well as Alvo's man. He did not understand the cause of the excitement which throbbed
in the young captive as if his heart would burst.

'Alvo! the Coward!' he cried in piercing tones,
and the lash of his whip cut the captive's cheek.

In the same instant . . . he felt that his throat
was grasped; his eyes became dizzy, he tottered,
and fell forwards. If it is possible to pay by
agony for sin, some part of a long reckoning
must have been discharged. But the deadly grasp
was dragged by main force from his throat; and
though all was still dark he felt again that he
could breathe. The other captives knew the
rest—had seen Ivlon's grip on Rudol, had seen
the band of Rema fall upon them both, had seen
Rudol left on the ground, a writhing heap, and
Ivlon in the hands of the rest, a prisoner. Ah!
it was over, their one faint gleam of hope, their
comrade's impatient deed had ruined them. And
he—if he had enjoyed an instant's vengeance, he
knew that now he must prepare for punishment

XI.

Ἐδίψησα, καὶ ἐποτίσατέ με.

RUDOL rose slowly.

He was still panting; there were red marks on his throat; he looked with half-blinded eyes to see if the soldiers laughed. This story of his fall would never be forgotten; for the rest of his life it would be told how a captive overcame him! One comfort remained—but still for a while he paused, for the convulsive motion of his throat would not suffer him to speak.

The sun was rising, and showed the plain wet with dew, and dotted with thorn-bushes, whilst in the distance were the outlines of mountains against the sky. All but Ivlon were standing; the Rema soldiers closing round him, and the two older captives as near him as they dared; Ascar pallid with anxiety and pity, and Uldic, with the countenance of a philosopher. Ivlon was quiet, sitting on the ground, his bound hands

loosely clasped, and his eyes looking in front of
him. He had once sewn a piece of charmed
gold into his doublet; he hoped it might help
him . . . he was in need of help.

'So!' cried Rudol in gasps; 'here is a captive
who would escape! Bring out the scourges.
He must be taught a lesson!' And the men,
nothing loth, produced or twisted scourges, whilst
Ascar trembled as he would not have trembled
for himself.

Ivlon, meanwhile, watched the men with steady
eyes; and, looking up at Uldic, smiled as children smile. He did not doubt that it would be
easy to be brave, for he had not had much experience of pain.

And now . . . his punishment was over. It had
been worse than he expected. It is terrible when
punishment is worse than expectation. He had
not cried out, had not asked for mercy, but still
he could not be sure that he was brave. Pale,
shivering as if he were shaken from head to foot,
he sat and looked stupidly in front of him. If
he could have died when he was in his master's
camp . . . he might have died without having
known such pain as this!

'Maravel,' Nardi said, 'we must do something
to his back. If these wounds do not heal—'

'Wait an instant,' cried Rudol. 'Bring out
slave's fetters, and fasten them on his ankles.

In future he shall not find it so easy to escape!'

A Rema brought the fetters, and stooped to fasten them; but raised himself, saying that the iron rings were too small. Rudol stamped his foot; and, seeing that he was determined, the man forced them on, exerting all his strength.

'And now,' Rudol cried, 'thou shalt be driven before me like a slave.'

The young captive raised heavy eyes, but did not move. A wan, piteous smile fluttered on his lips. It said, 'Thou hast hurt me so much that thou hast no power left.'

'Thou wilt not? Then thou shalt have more punishment. Give him some strokes on the backs of his feet. Will you obey me?'

The Rema had hesitated, but they now obeyed reluctantly, muttering that they had no wish to carry the prisoner. They struck—but their victim appeared not to feel the blows; his blank, leaden face could not now be moved by pain. For one instant the leader paused—and in that instant he caught sight of indignant features close to him.

'Aha, the young Estri!' cried Rudol, suddenly; 'there is no reason that the Estri should be spared. Listen, *you*,' to Ivlon, 'who sit there like a log, your carcase is valuable, or there should not be much left of it! But the young Estri'—and he proceeded to detail some of the foul forms of Rema punishment. 'Refuse to obey me, sit there an

instant longer, and the Estri shall swallow his eyes
before your face ! '

' Do nothing for me,' cried Ascar, instantly.

But, from the depth of his own anguish, Ivlon
heard the call ; and, howsoever borne down by
suffering, it was not in his nature to refuse to render
help.   He rose with an effort to his wounded feet ;
and Rudol realised that he was able to subdue him.
It was in *his* nature to make use of that knowledge
in order to inflict yet another humiliation.

' So ! thou wouldst save the Estri ?   Then go
down upon thy knees.   On thy knees !   Kneel to
me, or the Estri shall die for it.'

Ivlon trembled, wavered, hot with shame and
indecision ; but, as they seized Ascar, he sank
upon his knees.

The Rema laughed loudly ; they had not expected such submission, and it was natural that
they should receive it with contempt.   The great
face of Uldic flushed with indignation, moved for
the first time since his captivity.

' I did not desire it,' cried Ascar angrily.   ' I
wish no man to be sacrificed for me.   Swallow my
eyes yourself, Maravel ; and enjoy the taste of
them ! '

His imperfect accent made the Rema laugh·
Rudol laughed with them, almost with good-
humour.   Meanwhile, Ivlon, tottering, scarcely
able to support himself, leaned with closed eyes

against the tall stem of a thorn bush. Uldic drew
near him, his great face still flushed with wrath,
whose passion could be heard through the low
tones of his voice.

' Thou dost kneel to a Rema ! '

' Do not be angry,' Ivlon moaned. ' Uldic, say
thou art sorry for me.'

' It is all thy fault.'

' Still say thou art sorry. . . . At least I hurt his
throat.'

' That did us no good. I cannot understand
thee.'

' No,' muttered Ivlon. ' And thou wilt not
understand me until thy blood is hot—or until
mine is cold.'

He turned away wearily ; but the Rema came to
him, and laid hold of him for an examination.

' Bring salt for his back,' cried Nardi. ' These *are*
wounds. If these mortify—the Leopard may
claw us if he dies.'

' And the young leader,' whispered one in Nardi's
ear.

' True,' said Nardi aloud. ' Well, at least we will
dress his wounds. We have given the fool such a
lesson that he will be afraid of us next time.'

' Try me ! ' cried Ivlon, but the Rema only
laughed ; and, dragging him to the ground, set to
work upon his wounds.

Even in the half-stunned condition of the captive,

the torture they gave was almost unbearable. His
fainting condition appeared to move the soldiers,
if not to pity, at least to seriousness.

'I do not see,' said the Rema who had fettered
the captive's ankles, 'how he can walk in these
especially since his feet are wounded,'

'A man could do it.'

'Hardly.   And a lad is not a man.'

Rudol's harsh voice now cried that the band
was to move forward.

The men appeared to be afraid or discontented ;
but they dared not rebel, and the march began
once more.   The endless march !   It would be
impossible to find words with which to describe its
agony.

For all day Ivlon was conscious of little else
but pain—dizzy, burning pain, which filled his eyes
and ears ; heightened by a delirium of thirst, only
for an instant slaked by the rare draughts of water
allowed at intervals.   Once he fell, fainting, and
they poured water on his head, but the waste of
water roused the fury of the Rema, who threatened
that unless he kept upon his feet he should be
granted no drops to relieve his fever.   It was in
the hope of water—the one hope left in life—that
he struggled on upon his bandaged, wounded feet,
whilst strange sounds echoed in his ears, shadows
moved before his eyes, the voices near him seemed

to come from far away ; whilst the sky was black, the thorn-flowers blurs of yellow, and Uldic moved in front of him, and Ascar by his side. He went on in darkness, absorbed by a delirium which could not blot out the consciousness of pain.

Ascar kept near him ; it was all that he could do. Wrath, shame, and pity filled the Estri's heart. So this was another, this was a crowning instance to prove that the gods were unfit to rule the world ! What did the gods care? They looked down from their heaven and saw captives beaten, and helpless wives ill-treated, whilst *They* shone in the stars—they were in the hunting-grounds—no, in the cold deep Silence into which no voice can enter. After all, what does it matter, happiness or misery, the time comes to die, and have done with it ? And yet, far away, there was still the Alidrah where he might again have his bride, his wedding-night. . . . Some words fluttered ceaselessly :

'Help us, we are wretched. In mercy—in *Thy* mercy—lead us to our country.'

They floated into the silence of the plain, and he went on silently by Ivlon's side.

So that day passed ; and they could see in front of them the Rema mountains, distinct against the sky—the sunset came again with a flood of gold, and lying down on the ground, they tried to sleep. Ivlon had no sleep, however, and was of strange colours the next morning ; his face yellow, his lips blue, and his eyes set in dark circles whilst his head was inclined to sink forward on his breast, and his knees trembled as if he had the ague. The Rema bestowed all sorts of curses on him, and muttered that now they would be compelled to carry him. But Rudol saw no such necessity.

'Let him walk,' said the Maravel; 'he will walk fast enough if his share of water depends on it.'

Rudol was in high spirits. For the first time in his life he was tasting a vengeance which satisfied himself—the more so, doubtless, since each pang of his young victim was a weapon by which the young leader too was wounded. Ah! if the time came for Alvo to take vengeance—but then the old Maravel no longer shielded Alvo—the time might come, rather, when it would be possible to treat him as his favourite was being treated now. Rudol often imagined that he was striking Alvo—always with the understanding that Alvo's hands would then be bound.

'Aha,' he cried, as he rode up to his captive, 'he is not brisk now! We have bent his head at last!'

Ivlon held up his head with all the pride he had; and the Rema shouted that 'the lad was still impudent.'

'Then he shall have no water with the morning meal;' and satisfied with his sentence, the Maravel rode away.

'Of all the young fools!' Nardi muttered apart to Ivlon. 'Is it not possible even to *pretend* that you are humble?'

'I am thirsty. Will you give me water?'

Nardi laughed, and moved further off. If the lad died of fever it was no concern of his. He could say that he had fulfilled his duty to his master, if the time ever came to meet Maravel Alvo's wrath.

So that morning passed, and they came close to the hills, and halted. With delirious longing Ivlon saw them open jars and skins. Then the turn of the prisoners came, Ascar's first, Uldic's after him; and then at last—at last—they placed a bowl of water in his hands. For one instant he raised his head, and his eyes shone with delight; then he stooped to the water.

'Take it away from him,' said Rudol.

They took it from him. The water fell to the ground. For the first instant he was stunned, looking down with a stupid gaze. Then suddenly, he broke into the wildest laughter and crying, which rang terribly through the silence of the band. Even the Rema shuddered and shrank back, almost inclined to turn away their faces. Ivlon's knees gave way, and he fell down on the ground. He lay there, a quivering mass rather than a man.

Then one stepped forward, the Rema who had

fastened the fetters. His face was flushed, but he gave no other sign of fear.

'Maravel, he is only a boy. You are cruel.'

Rudol was too much astonished to be angry. He muttered that the cub must be taught manners, and rode on. The Rema pulled Ivlon from the ground, and dragged him on; telling him that if he were good he should have water in the evening. But the evening was far away, and Ivlon at an end of strength; he could not even submit to their handling, but sobbed and laughed deliriously. His condition was so terrible that before the evening came they halted beneath a rock, that he might rest. Ascar, in an agony, had tried to plead for him; but had been silenced by blows, and not permitted to walk near him. In all the wretchedness experienced by the captives they had never known such an afternoon as this.

Changes were at hand, however. As they lay beneath the rock, against which Ivlon leaned, with the soldiers round him, there came whispers that other Rema had arrived, and that Maravel Rudol had gone forward to them. Then, before the band had time to express its wonder, there suddenly appeared a small figure with a hatchet; and starting up, all the Rema rushed to it, and seized the new-comer with embracing arms. From their rough caresses little Lipsus—it was Lipsus

—struggled with all the strength he could command.

'Let go,' he cried in a shrill voice. 'My hatchet shall wound you! I tell you, let go of both of us. We will strike you! You will hear all the news when the Maravel comes back. I have only an instant, and I must see my prisoner.'

'*Your* prisoner,' cried the band; but the little Rema answered firmly,—

'The man I wounded—whom my hatchet wounded. He stands against the rock; I know him by his yellow hair. Ah!' He started, and for an instant said no more.

'He looks different,' said Lipsus, gravely.

'No wonder,' said the Rema.

'What have you done to his feet?'

'We cut them open with our scourges.'

'And his back also?'

'Ah! you should see his back.'

'And Maravel Rudol commands this,' muttered Lipsus.

'The fool tried to escape. He deserved punishment.'

'Truly,' said Lipsus. But he added, still more gravely: 'When I am a Maravel I will not ill-treat my prisoners.'

The band echoed with derision,—

'When Lipsus is Maravel!' but the little Rema paid no attention to them.

'This is nothing,' said one. 'It is what prisoners must expect. But it is a shame to give a man no water. He has had none to-day.'

With a sudden movement of his head, Lipsus looked up once more towards the prisoner. Then, suddenly, flinging his hatchet over his shoulder, with the shrill cry peculiar to him, he rushed away. The band looked after him, laughing; and with varying shades of scorn, pronounced that Lipsus would never be a Maravel.

'Only devils,' they said, quoting a familiar Rema proverb, 'can hope to win Maravel Ursan's love.'

Lipsus came round the rock, and cried to them,—

'Nadvin has come with two mules' burden of ornaments. The men who are near him are buying everything. Will you not go? I will watch the prisoners.'

The men started up. Moscar—the most merciful who, alone of the band, had once spoken for the captive—fixed his eyes on Lipsus with a singular expression; but he did not speak, and the band soon disappeared. It was evident from their exclamations of delight, that the arrival of Nadvin was a great event.

Then Lipsus came to Ivlon, drawing a rude flask from his breast.

'Stoop,' he said in a hoarse whisper, 'stoop and drink. It is only water, I could bring thee nothing

else.   Ah! make haste, drink quickly before
Maravel Rudol comes.'

Ivlon's mind was bewildered, but he understood the words.   He stooped, and the cold water
touched his burning lips.   One draught — one
short draught !—and then Lipsus was laid hold
of, and the rest of the water fell, wasted, to the
ground.

'Did I not understand thee ?' Moscar cried.
'At least I will save *thy* back from Maravel
Rudol.'

He swung Lipsus, hatchet and all, into his
arms ; and carried him away, regardless of his
struggles.   In a few instants, however, he returned
alone ; and after a moment's thought, approached
the captives.   •

'We are not all as Maravel Rudol,' he muttered
earnestly to Ivlon.   'Thy master has fought for
the Rema ; it is a shame to treat thee thus.   I have
vowed to be obedient—' his dark face was per-
turbed.   'If there were anything I could do for
thee—'

'There is !' cried Ivlon, 'and there is no
danger in it ! Place thy hand on my breast.
Dost thou feel the Rema charm ?   Take that, and
give it for me to the Rema Lipsus.   Tell him,' he
added with a quivering voice, 'that I pray to
the gods to give him water to drink when he is
thirsty.'

The effort of pronouncing the few words was too great, and with a moan he fell, fainting, to the ground. Moscar, in terror, summoned all the Rema, for it seemed as if death had set their victim free. They hastened to him, chattering, loaded with ornaments, and with them the dark-faced Nadvin and his mules. Rudol and Lipsus, however, were not with them ; and, observing the absence of the Maravel, Ascar felt a throb of hope. If the captives might only be allowed a little peace before they reached the land of the Rema . . . and the end.

XII

Then through the darkness of that darkest night
Our hands reached, clasped each other.

WAS this the end? It was evening; they had
halted beneath a rock; the last halt permitted
before they reached the Leopard's Den. Beneath them the red sunset shone over a barren
country, from which barren hills seemed to rise
and swell like waves. This was the Land of the
Rema; the march was nearly over; some rest
must be at hand, even if it were only the rest
of death. Meanwhile, down a deep defile there
went with tinkling bells the departing footsteps
of Nadvin and his mules.

Ascar lay and pondered. Since Rudol had
left the band, both himself and his fellow-captives
had been treated mercifully; for the grave, surly
Rema official who had been left in command had
been alarmed by the condition of the prisoners.
From these fears, and from the kindness of the
little, bright-eyed Nadvin, it had followed that

Ivlon and himself had been bound upon the
mules, that they had been revived with sufficient
food, even wine, and that in this leisure some days
of rest had passed. Days of dreams! during which
Ascar had been chiefly conscious of the continual
tinkle of the mule-bells in his ears. And now
Nadvin was gone, and on himself and the other
prisoners lay already the shadow of an approaching
end.

Ascar raised his head. Seated with his back
against the rock was Uldic, utterly tired, but brave
and stolid. At a little distance stood Ivlon,
leaning against the rock to support himself, with
his eyes on a mouse which had just come from a
crevice. These men had saved him, they had suffered with him, and yet how few words he had exchanged with them! And now—in the presence of
death— With a sudden impulse, he moved forward
a few steps, and stood at Ivlon's side. The young
captive turned to him a sunken face; and then,
bending his eyes to the ground, was motionless.

Some Rema passed, glancing and muttering.

'They are talking of us,' said Ascar, amazed at
the effort that the few words required.

Ivlon looked at him again, and on his haggard
face rose a weary bitterness which at last stirred
his lips.

'We are worth looking at,' he said—'the faultless
Uldic, who never commits an error, or forgives one

in another—the fine Estri Ascar who in the Land
of Spirits itself will not talk unless he has Estria to
talk with him.'

He bent his head, and pulled grass out of the
rock, which he kept twisting with weary, restless
fingers.

The Estri was angry, but at that moment other
sensations were too strong for even his anger to
subdue them.

'If that is Ascar,' he asked gently, 'what is
Ivlon?' And with his bound hands he touched
his companion's arm.

Ivlon looked round on him, amazed, and his lips
trembled; but he did not move from his companion. After a while he spoke, with his eyes
looking far away, as if they were attracted by the
deep glow of the sunset,—

'I! I!' he said, I am nothing, nobody—I am
the youngest of the Ninety—I am Alvo's shield-
bearer. I might be—' he paused—'Estri Ascar's
friend—for a while—if he will. I am his fellow-
captive, whether he will or not.'

'Let us be friends,' cried Ascar eagerly, unable
to resist this gentle nature any longer.

Their hands clasped, and the Estri thought irresistibly of the moment when he had touched the
hands of the wizard's son. This face was not that
of Olbri, pale, keen and critical; and yet—not
less worthy of love—   ·

'Why, they make friends!' cried a Rema.

The young men looked at each other, and their laughter rang in peals. For the first time the Estri fully understood that cheerfulness is possible where there is companionship. He did not forget the lesson, even when they were separated, and the Rema had punished the unusual mirth. Uldic shrugged his broad shoulders. The young captives deserved their stripes. For himself, he desired neither mirth nor companionship.

Ah, the new friendship! Through the darkness of the night the two young prisoners, pleased as those who have found a treasure, seized each opportunity permitted by their captors to draw near and whisper a few words to each other. They were tired, the night was long, there were few stars in the sky; it was strange how much comfort could be found in such foolish words. Strange, too, that to Ascar the forms of Ered and Olbri seemed to be closer than they had been before. If the Gods were angry . . . but then the Gods, who have heavenly wisdom, must know of some country to which *all* men belong. Under the stern hand of captivity the young Estri himself was losing prejudices.

And now — the end! Through a beautiful summer evening he was dragged up steep paths towards the Leopard's Den, too faint to observe the ways, to look back for his companions, or even to have any anxiety about his fate. Some consciousness he had of a black overhanging rock, and then that too failed, and for a while he knew no more. And then . . . he raised his head to find himself in a dark passage, with Rema near him, and Uldic and Ivlon by his side.

Ivlon was seated on the ground, and some blood from his wounded feet was trickling slowly into the crevices. Uldic, for his part, leaned against the wall, and with closed eyes had composed himself for sleep. They had laid Ascar on a seat cut in the wall, from which he started now that his consciousness returned. He could see the dark passage, dank with clinging mist, the torches on the walls, his two companions . . .

' Where are we ? ' he cried.

Ivlon answered with surprise,—

' Hast thou forgotten ? We are in the Leopard's Den.'

' Is the march over ?

' It is over, Estri Ascar.'

' And now—will they kill us ? '

' They have not told us what they will do.'

Ivlon smiled. In that strange place his wan face was familiar, and Ascar dropped to the ground and clung to him. They crouched together, with their arms round each other ; for their hearts were made tender by the thought of death.

'Didst thou see the sunset, Ascar?'

'I do not know.'

'Thou didst not look! And we may never see another! Ascar, lean on my shoulder and sleep. We may never sleep again.'

'Or always sleep,' said Ascar. 'Ivlon, art thou afraid to die?'

'I cannot tell. I should be glad to have no feet. My wounds broke open to-night, and they beat me before they carried me. Ascar, the march is over!'

'It is over,' said Ascar. 'And we shall be together if we die.'

They clung together, supporting each other on the ground. The Rema, at some distance, stood and looked at them. Uldic snored.

'How wise Uldic is!' said Ivlon, laughing. 'He is much wiser than either you or I.'

He tossed his curls, almost as if he were light-hearted.

'Sleep, Ascar. I am in too much pain to sleep.'

Ascar clung to him with closed eyes, but could not sleep. He seemed to be still marching on the endless plain. . . . And now came the tramp of feet; a band of men approached with torches. Had they come to lead them to death? Ah! at least the march was over! . . . The footsteps echoed, came close. They were in the midst of a band of soldiers. The prisoners rose with weary

movements to their feet. Their eyes were bandaged, and they were led away. This was the last
march, this would be the end !

And now ! They stood together, their bandages
removed. Behind them were the rude stone steps
they had descended. Beneath them a stone had
been moved, and they looked down into what
seemed a black, unfathomable gulf.

A horror seized Ascar, and shuddered through
his limbs. He could almost have knelt and implored the Rema to have mercy. But no time was
allowed. They released the prisoners' hands and
feet, and lowered them, one by one, into the
gulf. The turn of the Estri came first ; and, as he
touched the stones below, he let go the cords, and
sank upon the ground. None could see him
in the darkness, or know that in that moment
the last remnant of courage had deserted him.
Then Uldic was near him, then Ivlon ; and
then with a sullen sound the stone rolled back,
and all light was gone from them. They
grasped each other. In that overwhelming instant that involuntary grasp was the only comfort
left.

'Ered !' cried Ascar.

The word seemed the last cry, the last effort that
he would make before he died.

Ivlon muttered, 'Estri Alvo,' and Uldic groaned

heavily. They let go of each other, and sank upon the ground. Then Ivlon sprang to his feet with a peal of laughter which made strange echoes through the darkness of the gulf.

'Ah, see!' he cried. 'I am the best man after all. I will crawl through this blackness, and reach the end of it. Come, Uldic, Ascar. What! you will not move! Then I will get through my adventure by myself.'

He moved away, crawling, for he could not walk. From the distance his voice was heard saying that 'there was mud.' Again, still more dolefully, that 'the mud was deep.' And, then, suddenly, it rang out as of old : 'I have found a large stone!'

Uldic heaved himself in response. Ascar still lay with his face upon his arms. But the voice from the distance came almost joyfully,—

'I have found food—water. They do not mean to starve us! See,' cried Ivlon, 'here are cords to lower food. They mean us to live for the present at any rate. And when Estri Alvo hears. . . . We may find a path which will lead from this dungeon to the Fair Country.'

To the Fair Country!

The words murmured in Ascar's ears as, crouched on the ground, he ate and drank with his companions, as, the meal ended, he looked with them for a dry place, and lay down at last to rest by Ivlon's side. They clung to each other in the unfathomable darkness. Would they ever see the light of the sun again?

'Ivlon,' whispered Ascar, 'I am thinking of my wife.'

'And I,' whispered Ivlon, 'of Estri Alvo's camp. Ascar, dost thou pray to the Good Spirits?'

'I do not know. Dost thou think the Good Spirits ever come down here?'

'I know not,' said Ivlon; 'but we shall learn here in the darkness. We shall become wiser in darkness than we have ever been in daylight. Ascar, this prison is cold, but we will keep each other warm. The march is over. Let us sleep.'

And they slept.

THE CAMP OF ALVO.

᾿ οἱ γὰρ τοιαῦτα λέγοντες ἐμφανίζουσιν ὅτι πατρίδα ἐπιζητοῦσι.

Non enim uno modo sacrificatur transgressoribus angelis.

XIII.

Oh, stormy prime, so beautiful
   With fierce delight, ecstatic pain,
Spending and being spent, no lull,
   No pause, no count of loss or gain,
Ere with tired feet thou come to tread
   The blood-stained field of ended wars—

Wherefore do ye spend your labour for that
   which satisfieth not?

WE are drawing near to our first halting-place, but there is one scene which we must visit first. We have been in the Fair Country, and over the dreary plain, with Ursan and Rudol in the camp, with Envar and Maro in the Council, with Ascar in the dungeon, with Ered on the Escola. But we have yet to make the acquaintance of the leader with whose destiny all these others are entwined, who has at least made himself of so much consequence that it is impossible for him to rise or fall alone. Until we have looked on his face with our own eyes

we will pronounce no judgment on his worth or
worthlessness. The voices of friends and of
enemies have spoken; let us now see the camp
and the camp's master for ourselves.

It is noon, and blue sky looks down on Alvo's
camp. The soldiers have resigned themselves to
their mid-day sleep. Through all the wide space,
dotted everywhere with tents, there is scarcely a
sound to be heard, or a human being to be seen.
At intervals, at the outskirts where the sentinels
are placed, an occasional footstep tells that a
sentinel is changed. Unhappy is the fate of the
replacer if he does not reach his post in time, for
Maravel Alvo rules with an iron hand.

The camp is well defended. It is on a natural
platform, behind which rise precipitous hills, whose
few defiles are guarded. In front the ground drops
sharply to a level of smooth green turf, pleasant to
the eye, but in reality a dangerous marsh; whilst
at the sides the safe, gentle slopes are defended
by stakes and ditches—the whole semi-circle being enclosed by one great ditch which, sweeping
round the marsh, joins the hills on either hand.
Enclosed in this manner by ditches, hills, and
marshes, the camp may almost be deemed impreg-
nable.

Within is an order characteristic of a leader
whose men say that 'you can tell the ditch where

he has lain by the care with which the reeds have
been disturbed.' In the centre, dividing the camp
into two parts, is the exercise-ground. Behind it,
on a slope that overlooks the whole camp, is the
tent of the Maravel. The right side of the camp
is devoted to the Rema. On the left are the mixed
tribes, and the Ninety Exiles. At the back are
kept stores of provisions and animals. Everything
is in order in each part of the space. No sounds
of dice can be heard, no drunken songs ; the fierce,
brawling camp by the Tordrade might behold its
contrast here. And it is even possible that a keen
observer, remembering the devotion of the men of
Ursan to their leader, might ask whether the contrast were complete in all respects. For, marvellous as is the harmony produced, this military des-
potism whic savours of anxiety.

However that may be, the soldiers are quiet now
in their tents after a morning more pleasant and
excitable than usual. For a band of Karngria
have arrived, entering the camp that day, in the
company of a few stragglers from the neighbourhood. Amongst these last, who were promptly
discovered and dismissed, was observed a man
with a horrible scar on his face, whose whole
appearance was so unusual that two or three
determined to detain and question him. When
sought, however, he was nowhere to be found, and
it was supposed that he had departed with the rest.

And now—the camp is asleep beneath the grey hills, which rise behind it massively until their outlines are framed by the blue sky. Not a cloud stirs in the sky, not a leaf moves in the woods. It would seem as if even the earth itself were asleep. But, soft! in the ditch below the camp we can observe a figure stirring. What is its errand in the midst of silence?

It moves swiftly, noiselessly, with the motion of a cat, scarcely making the branches crack, or the leaves rustle, not to be seen through the bushes unless any one above should take the trouble to push them aside and peer down into the depth. And now it has reached the point where the ditch becomes a ravine, below the tents inhabited by the Karngria. And still it goes onwards—then suddenly it stops, and crouches down noiselessly beneath the leaves.

It has not stopped an instant too soon. There is a clear space in the ravine; and there, on a fallen log, two companions are seated, pouring out greeting and welcome to each other, as friends who have not met for some length of time. One is a Rema, with the pale grey eyes, the sharply cut features of the best tribe of his race; the other, brown, irregular-faced, with dark flashing glance, has the bony chin and large mouth of the Karngria. Two good specimens of their respective tribes are these, with little trace of their nations' more sinister qualities; and, as the concealed figure listens to their eager words, his face becomes dark from inward bitterness. He has no companion, this man of disfigured face, who, with ear to the leaves, is listening cautiously.

'Tell me now of thy doings,' cries the Karngri, for until this moment he has been pouring out his own. 'Since we parted after a plunder-expedition, and thou wert sent here, what has been happening to thee?'

'I—have been living here,' answers the Rema, indifferently. 'How long hast thou been in the camp?'

'Since the morning.'

'Hast thou seen *him* yet?'

'The young leader? Only for an instant. He came out of his tent and said a few words to us.'

'Didst thou not think him altered?'

'I had only seen him twice—once, at a council, leaning on Maravel Ursan's shoulder; and once, after a skirmish, when his wounds were being dressed. He is as pale now as he was then.'

'He has been ill—he is ill,' said the Rema. 'And he allows himself no rest.'

The Karngri laughed and laid himself on his back, that he might dip his fingers into the purple cup of a flower.

'He is not wise,' he said.

But the Rema looked at him with the keen, thin-lipped smile peculiar to his race.

'My friend,' he said, 'thou shouldst learn to know the camp. There are here the Gortona, the Effar, and the Nira, and Alvo's own band, and your countrymen, and mine. The Gortona hate the Effar, the Effar and the Nira hate the Karngria, the Karngria '—he smiled—'hate the Rema, and as for the Rema they hate all except themselves. And each tribe is governed by its own laws, and there is nothing each set of soldiers longs for so much as it longs to be at the throats of all the rest.'

The Karngri sat up in surprise.

'Then what keeps you from each other's throats ? '

'Only the young leader.'

'Then he is a commander after all.'

'He is a commander.' (The word signified *able to command*.) 'I never believed it till I came to his camp.'

'But what can he do ? '

'How can I tell thee what he does ? I will tell what he will do when he first speaks to you. He will smile at you from under his long eyelashes, and will whisper a few soft words in the language of the Karngria.'

'Bah, that is nothing ! Tell me of his qualities.'

'He is the handsomest fellow in the camp,' said the Rema, laughing.

'And that is nothing!'

'I am not sure that it is nothing, since thou wilt not paint thy face after the manner of thy countrymen. Ah! thou art blushing— What more can I tell thee of him? In the same instant he can be a wise man and a fool. He will go out without armour, and fight till he streams with blood, and then almost shed tears because an insect stings him.'

'And yet thou believest in him?' cried the Karngri, with contempt.

'A man must believe in his leader.'

'Thou hast not lost thy old folly yet! Why must we believe in our leaders?'

The Rema spoke seriously,—

'Friend, there is no man without some qualities. This man is mad, for instance, but he has fire from the gods. And we must believe in our leaders as we believe in the gods of our country—' he paused for an instant looking up to the blue sky.

'Because we have found no better.'

The man under the bushes drew himself a little closer. The Karngri threw an arm across the knees of his friend.

'Ah! do not become too wise for me,' he murmured. He added: 'Thou hast told of the leader. What do the soldiers think of him?'

'They—they hate him, are ready to destroy

him. But he is able to subdue them for the present.   Then he has his own band near him.'

'A brave army !   Ninety men.'

'They are the best soldiers in the camp.'

'Better soldiers than the Rema ? '

'They are better trained.'

'Thou canst speak against thy countrymen ? '

'Yes,' cried the Rema; with light in his pale
eyes, 'because my countrymen will be masters of
all in time.   They can wait.'

'And mine are impatient,' cried the Karngri.
But, at least, they are not false or cruel. . . . Ah,
forgive me, for I am so much in need of thee. . .
Tell me if Alvo's men love him.'

'More than each one loves his life.'

'And does he love them ? '

'He has a folly for the youngest.   He will sacrifice them all for the sake of the Fair Country. . .
I must see to my men.'

'Wait an instant,' cried the Karngri.   'The
hardest question is last.   Hast *thou* any love for
him ? '

The Rema paused.

'He is a son of the Alidrah,' he muttered.   'No
Rema can love him.'

'Except Ursan.'

'Except Ursan,' said the Rema.

But his companion was not satisfied.

'If he were not of the Alidrah ? '

Again the Rema paused, as if the question were difficult.

'I should think him,' he said at last, slowly and with emphasis, 'a fool who will lead to death better men than himself. Let us go.'

They rose, stumbling in the bushes, catching their feet in tangled grass, so close to the unseen watcher that he laid his hand on his breast. But they did not touch him; they climbed lightly up through the bushes, whispering and laughing to each other, and went on into the camp. As their voices died away the watcher rose silently, and came to stand for an instant in the clear space where they had been. For that instant the sunlight shone on his distorted, haggard face—then he dropped on his knees, and crawled through the grass again. As he proceeds with a stealthy, noiseless motion, we will enter the tent of the leader of whom we have heard so much.

In Alvo's tent are two men, unlike in appearance; a burly giant, whose great features are red with passion, and a thin man with pale face and dark, shining eyes. It is his voice that is speaking—hard, tremulous, vibrating, and yet so low that only its clearness leaves it audible.

'I know why thou art angry. It is because I reproved thee before the Rema. I will reprove thee again to-morrow, and will punish thee again.

Thou wilt not learn the exercise that every Rema knows. And I will not have my men beaten by the Rema.'

'They are beaten sometimes, Estri,' muttered the giant sullenly.

'Then my men shall suffer for it,' Alvo answered.

He turned away as he spoke, with a sigh as if he were exhausted, and leaned against one of the posts that supported the tent. The giant moved sullenly from him; but before he had taken many steps he turned as if his passion could be restrained no longer.

'Estri, dost thou know what the Rema say of us?'

He stopped, appalled by the fire in Alvo's eyes. But the gleam was gone in an instant.

'What is it?' asked Alvo, with a faint, hard smile. 'It must be true if the Rema say it.'

He looked at his soldier steadily, and his glance had such compelling power that the man went on speaking, although with difficulty.

'They say, Estri, that there are no men in the camp who have such hard training, such severe laws as ours. They say that thou wouldst not dare to impose such laws on others, but that thou knowest we are afraid of thee—'

He stopped, panting with mingled dread and passion, and Alvo continued looking at him with a glance as keen as the point of an unsheathed knife.

'Go on.'

'Estri—Estri—'

'Thou hast nothing more to say? Then I will speak—*I*—once for all, as I have never spoken to thee before. When I took thee with me to win the Fair Country, did I promise thee an easy life; did I promise thee wine or women, the dice that the Rema love, the fire-wine of the Karngria, or soft beds, or dainty hours? Do *I* have an easy life, do I rest by day or night, I, your chosen leader, who work for you as for myself? I have kept my promises; and now my soldier comes to me, and tells me that only fear keeps my own men at my side.'

He turned away his face. His voice was low and cold.

'I will not punish thee; I release thee from thy vows. Go. Return to the mountains. I need not speak to thee again.'

He stood still, motionless, with his face still turned away. The giant looked at him, bewildered, miserable, shifting the weight of his great form from one foot to the other. He moved away a few steps, he came back to his place; he stood, quivering, with his eyes fixed on his master. All at once he cried, '*Estri!*' and, flinging himself upon his knees, he seized the leader's arm with his hands. Great, blubbering sobs burst from him as with a grasp strong as iron he pressed the arm of his master to his breast.

Had Alvo expected that moment? As now at last he turned his face it did not display the least trace of resentment; it had broken into tremulous smiles in eyes and lips which gave it the mischievous expression of a child. And as, without attempting to release his captured arm, he bent down and touched the giant's head with his other hand, the movement was as caressing and as gentle as that of a beautiful woman who grants her admirer an embrace. No doubt he knew that the moment for sugar-plums had come, for the young leader understood his men.

'Why, Sidric,' he murmured, in a voice gentle as his face, 'so miserable? I have given thee thy freedom. But thou dost not wish to leave us; and I—I am not angry any longer. It hurts me too much to be angry with my men. Get up. A man must not remain too long on his knees. We must learn to be better children, thou and I.'

'Sidric,' he said, more gravely, as the giant stood before him, with sunken head and appearance of defeat, 'believe me, it would not be to our advantage if we relaxed the training which makes us the best soldiers in the camp. We shall have full need of every discipline before we are able to win the Fair Country. Still—this exercise—'

'Ah, this exercise,' moaned Sidric, with a despair that proceeded from the lowest depths of his breast; and, indeed, his master was sufficiently aware that this particular follower was without capacity.

Alvo stood considering, whilst the giant watched his bright eyes with the expression with which a dog looks at its master.

'Only a few days ago I taught a Rema,' Alvo said, ' and the Rema cannot complain if I teach my own men as well. To-morrow will be a hard day —oh! a hard day—but I will find some time in which to attend to thee. Come to my tent before the dawn and wake me, and I will explain thy exercise before the day begins . . . And now, go ; I am tired, and must have a moment's rest ; and when Osymn comes I must be alone with him.'

He laid his hands on the arm of Sidric, that he might push him gently away, but still with a move-ment that seemed like a caress ; and as the giant slouched off slowly, awkwardly, his eyes smiled from under his long eyelashes. Yet, when he was left, the smile faded from his face, which changed like that of an actor whose part is done, or that of one who has forgotten a burden of anxiety which returns as soon as he finds himself alone. With dropped head, and weary lips, he stood leaning against the pole, his arms hanging and his eyes absorbed in thought. As the young leader waits we will take advantage of the occasion to learn his face and his story for ourselves.

X I V.

Whate'er he did was done with so much ease,
In him alone 'twas natural to please.

A man so various, that he seemed to be
Not one, but all mankind's epitome.

A STRANGE face, on which a strange history has
been written, this face of the young leader, the
Leader Beautiful, the Maravel who, in proving
the presents of the gods, has learned to turn his
beauty into power ! So variable is this face that
its changes are bewildering ; and yet through all
changes it has steadfast qualities—a young face,
sorrowful, mischievous, capricious, but never desti-
tute of a leader's genius. Where has Alvo learnt
all those varying expressions, like those of a gem
that has been cut to many sides ; what hard fate
has made him so careworn in his youth, and lighted
his eyes with such uncertain hope ? A close
observer must own that they can have been no
easy times which have fashioned this singular jewel
of the Exiles, that hard probation must have trained

this brilliant leader, the favourite of Ursan, the darling of the Gods. Leaving the young sunken face, careworn and brilliant, with a leader's keenness, a woman's loveliness, let us look on the past, for that will tell us of the present, and may even afford some means by which the future can be judged.

This was Alvo's story.

His mother had been a slave, bought by the only descendant of the chief family of the Exiles, who was so much attracted by her terror and her beauty that he wedded her in secret the same night that he bought her. The nobleman, however, became tired of his toy, and left his bride to depart on a long excursion ; and it was during his absence that the unfortunate maiden fell into the hands of the Rema, who again sold her for a slave. Left alone, helpless, inexperienced, threatened by the worst dangers that loveliness can bring, the terrified slave made one desperate attempt to escape to her husband before her child was born. She was discovered, brought back, and the rich merchant who was her master, who until that moment had loaded her with gifts, was seized with fury at her ingratitude . . . For shame, even his officials made some attempt at last to help her, but with the morning, and the birth of her child, she died, leaving it a matter of little marvel that her son should be of a sickly constitution from his birth. And perhaps the young leader owed more than sickliness to the circumstances which attended his entrance into the world.

For the time he was spared. One of the officials of the merchant, who had pitied the mother's agony, took possession of the child; and when it was granted to his keeping as a present, caused it to be conveyed privately to the Exiles. These received it coldly; and its father, who in a distant country at last heard news of the fate of his wife and child, was so overwhelmed with despair that he would not return to his home, but went out to battle with the mountain tribes. Long afterwards, one who saw him on the eve of a great battle, reported that he looked altered, old and careworn, that he spoke sorrowfully of the life which he had wasted, and of the countrymen who had honoured him as their chief.

'They loved me,' he said, 'and I have done no good to them. Tell my son from me that he must win the Fair Country.'

He turned away after saying these few words. The next day he was killed.

'A father's last command,' say the Estria, 'is as binding as an oath.' It was the misfortune of Alvo to be bound, even from his childhood.

'If I had no wish to regain my country,' he told Ursan, 'it would not be possible to forget my father's words.'

Meanwhile, his childhood had been spent amongst the Exiles, who had loved his father, but who had little love for him—the slave's child, sickly, feeble, ready to cry if he was touched, with a shrinking from pain that was almost a disease.

' I remember those days,' he said long afterwards to Ursan, ' and the grey-haired men who punished me to make me brave.'

They could not make him brave ; at that time nothing seemed more certain than that the slave's child was without noble qualities.

And then . . . there came to the place a Rema merchant who was immediately struck with the beauty of the boy, and, after loading him with sweetmeats and rich garments, promised that if he would leave the Exiles he should be treated like a prince. The Exiles, who heard of these promises, were furious, and placed a close watch on the son of the Alvoi ; but Alvo, whose childish fancy had been attracted by the gifts, escaped from restraint one night, and fled to the Rema tents. It was a child's choice ; but in the after years the Exiles never forgot it, or forgave.

Meanwhile, punishment followed. The pretty boy, once a captive, was not fed on sweetmeats or treated like a prince ; on the night of his escape he was sold to a rough master, and carried off, weeping and struggling, to the mountains.

'On that day,' said Alvo, 'I learned to understand the love of men who give sweetmeats and
promises.'

He disappeared, and of all those who had known
him there was not one who imagined that he would
be ever seen again.

The long winter passed, however, and some
travellers in the summer spoke of a bright-eyed
boy they had observed amongst the mountain-
lads, recognised by one as the same whom he had
once seen in the winter, crouching over a fire as
if the cold would kill him. This was indeed Alvo,
trained and educated to be a good climber and
an active slave, although he bore marks upon his
back and breast which showed with what difficulty
the lessons had been learned. In spite of these
scars, and of the winter's cold, the mountain-life
had been valuable.

'I used to like to search for eggs in dangerous
places,' he told Ursan, 'though often it was a long
time before I dared to climb. I would try day
after day to reach some nest I chose, and each day
would come nearer, even if it were only by a tuft
of grass. And when I had some time for rest I
would climb as high as I dared, and lie down and
think of the Great Spirit, whose breath made
even me. I was always hungry, and covered with
bruises.'

'The boy was a strange creature,' said his

master, the *Old Wolf*, 'tame enough in his way, and yet with a fire-spirit. He was so different from others that one looked for him when he was gone.'

The speech does not sound unkindly ; and Alvo, on his part, never spoke bitterly of his old master.

' *He* never called me a coward,' Alvo said.

Their parting was characteristic. The tribe to which the Old Wolf belonged fell under the displeasure of the Rema, who issued a proclamation that all its slaves were free. On a winter morning the Old Wolf heard this command, but he determined not to speak of it till the evening, in order that the skilful fingers of his young slave might make for him a large net. It chanced, however, that Alvo, going out in the evening to the flocks, heard of his freedom from one of the mountain-lads. He went back, sat down by the fire without speaking, and began to untwist the net.

' What dost thou ? ' asked the Wolf.

' The work is mine, not thine,' said Alvo.

His master answered not a word. But when the net lay on the ground, a tangled cord, and Alvo silently rose, he went up to him,—

' These clothes are mine, not thine,' he said ; and, stripping him, turned him out into the cold of a winter's night.

' I found a hovel at last,' said Alvo, ' and wandered near it a long while, for I was ashamed. But I had kept my two charms in my mouth' (two gold charms which had belonged to his father and mother), 'and I went in at last, and with these bought clothes and food that I might be able to go down into the world.

Down into the beautiful world which held the Exiles, which held the Great Plain, and beyond it the Fair Country, which should now hold him, a young creature full of life, full of unknown genius, unsuspected powers! The first step, however, which he took in this unknown world, was one which might have destroyed all life and power for ever.

For, in the course of the long journey down the mountain, Alvo met a band of men with long robes and flowing beards, who accosted him kindly, seemed impressed by his appearance, and asked him many questions about himself and about his race. Priests of Beauty, they called themselves; and always whilst they spoke they looked curiously at him.

Alvo did not know—his inexperience had no means of knowing—that amongst the worst signs of those evil times were such priests as these, hidden in the shelter of the mountains, where they performed rites, falsely called religious. They told him stories of dreams and ceremonies, of spells by which demons were conquered, and the favour of the gods was won ; and his young imagination, easily kindled, dreamed of a path by which the Fair Country might be gained. The men received him with the utmost readiness, and quickly vanished into the mountains with their prize. In this manner Alvo disappeared for the second time. But of this period of his life he never spoke.

It did not last long. In the succeeding spring a boy might have been seen flying over mountain-paths, scarcely pausing for rest or sleep till he reached a valley, and a river, down which a company of men were travelling. Then, whilst he stood on the shore, imploring them to take him in their boat, and whilst they hesitated to burden themselves with a stranger, another company of men came out from the woods near the river, and claimed the fugitive. For since the night on which Alvo had escaped from the priests they had not ceased to pursue him night and day.

A conflict followed. With the wildest tears and prayers Alvo clung to the merchant to whom the boat belonged, promising to serve him for ever as his slave if only he might be delivered from the priests. The merchant was moved by the boy's beauty, had pity on his terror, and, moreover, was not unwilling to gain a valuable slave; he therefore drove back the priests with blows and curses, and received the fugitive into the boat. The priests went back, and by their influence with the Rema were able to wreak a bitter vengeance on the Exiles. But of this Alvo was ignorant.

He had duties to occupy him, for he was now again a slave, and slavery was a hard lot to one who had been free.

'My master was kind,' he told Ursan, 'and taught me how to handle weapons; but although I worked all day I could not always sleep at night. I thought that when my countrymen returned to the Fair Country, I should not be with them.'

For his dream grew with him.

The good-natured merchant, meanwhile, had so much liking for the boy that he would have set him free if he could have borne to part with him; and, on one occasion, when Alvo had saved him from a wild beast's grip, he even offered him his freedom, which was refused.

'It was not for that I risked my life,' said Alvo. 'I wanted to tell myself that I was brave.'

His young, proud nature had not been able to forget the reproach of cowardice which he had heard so often in his childhood.

Freedom was not long delayed. On the occasion of his marriage, the master of Alvo granted it to all his slaves; and when, as the most valuable he would have excepted Alvo, his young wife made supplication for the boy.

'I will grant him his freedom at thy wish,' he said, 'but I shall never have such a piece of merchandise again.'

'When shall we next see the lad?' she murmured, as the young slave knelt before her.

Her husband answered, laughing,—

'When the Exiles have returned.'

He had no knowledge that Alvo believed in that return, and his careless words filled the boy's eyes with tears. Alvo did not speak, however, and his tears passed unnoticed. He saluted his master and mistress, and departed. Once more he was free, and now at last he could return and learn from the exiles how to gain the Fair Country.

He did return.

'It was at the time of sunset,' he told Ursam . . 'I saw a few wretched hovels, a few miserable men ; and I heard them cursing the name of their young Estri, who had brought on them the vengeance of the Rema and the priests. And then, as I stood, trembling, a man who had seen my mother recognised me—for I have my mother's face—and they all shouted at me and called me slave and coward, and I was such a fool, and so sad I could not answer. Then a few who had loved my father saved my life, and took care of me during my sickness, for I was sick almost to death.'

His illness, indeed, had lasting consequences, for

it wasted the strength which the mountains had given him; and its immediate effect was to produce with tenfold force one of the periods of depression to which he was liable.

'And yet I had visions in those days,' he said to Ursan, 'and fires often seemed to dance before my eyes; and I could not tell if I were mad, or if the Great Spirit spoke to me. I used to lie on the ground, beneath the stars, and entreat the Great Spirit to teach me not to be a fool. For in those days all men scorned me, and I myself believed that there was nothing in me which did not deserve contempt.'

The delusion could not last long. It chanced that one day at a Council some man chose to taunt the young Estri with helplessness. Alvo stood up, and all at once his eyes flashed. The flame-spirit that was in him burned at last.

'Are you so certain?' he asked.

'Then lead us to the Alidrah. It is for you to command us.'

'Then I will command you.'

There was silence, and all men looked at the Estri, and at each other. From that moment the Estri knew himself. A beautiful moment but a dangerous is that when such knowledge first mingles with our dreams.

Alvo, however, was happy as he had never been before. His wild nature had awaked, and he mistrusted it no longer ; although he was as conscious of inexperience as of genius, and immediately resolved to educate himself. He left the Exiles, and joined the bands of Helos, who at that time were at war with the Karngria ; whilst the Exiles, once more bereaved of their chief noble, looked for him, as the Wolf had done, when he was gone. To Alvo, meanwhile, an important event occurred. He became acquainted with the Maravel of the Rema.

That was on this wise. In the company of a band of youths he had gone out upon an expedition. They had been ordered to advance to a certain place, but before they reached it they were surrounded by the enemy. The position was perilous ; it was impossible to go forward ; and the Helos accounted it a dishonour to retreat.

'We must retreat,' said Alvo. 'Give me the command, I will take the blame.

' Then you will be dishonoured.'

' I care not,' Alvo replied.

He took the command, and managed the retreat with so much skill that they passed undiscovered through the midst of the enemy. On their return, however, they were attacked with loud reproaches, and the whole shame rested on the stranger who had advised them to retreat. At that moment the Maravel of the Rema was near at hand, negotiating both with Helos and Karngria. He heard the story, and immediately wrote a message.

'Send to my camp this leader who retreats.'

The Helos were not inclined to dispute any wish from Ursan; and Alvo, expecting contempt, was taken to the Leopard's camp.

Alvo never forgot that day. Through the whole of a long morning he was left alone with the terrible old leader, looking into the pale eyes when he dared, and listening to the tones of a voice none could hear without being moved. Ursan gained from him the whole tale of the retreat, he was even anxious to hear its minutest details; but when the story was told he did not make a single comment, but remained silent, and seemed absorbed in thought. Then he said, 'Come, I will show you to my leaders;' and he looked into Alvo's downcast face and smiled.

Ursan's leaders remembered that day. They were lying on the ground, thinking of nothing less than their dreaded Maravel, when suddenly they started, as they heard his voice behind them.

'My friends, I bring you a young leader.'

Up they started in confusion, and saw by Ursan's side a boy—for so he seemed—with slight frame and drooping face, whose long, black eyelashes rested on cheeks crimson with blushes. In amazement they were silent; and Ursan, seeing that Alvo was distressed, came closer to him and laid

an arm across his shoulders. The resentment of
Rudol could not be restrained.

'Ah, Maravel,' he said, 'that is a maiden !'

Alvo drew his sword at once, but Ursan took it
from his hand.

'Pardon me,' he murmured, 'we leaders do not
fight;' and still looking at him, as if he were
interested : 'Come to my tent ; I have a word for
thee.'

He did not speak when they were together in
his tent ; but laid his hands on Alvo's shoulders,
and pierced him with his glance ; until Alvo, at
last unable to endure it, raised his head timidly,
and their eyes met. Strange eyes had the old
Maravel, eyes that *knew ;* for the first time Alvo
met a glance that understood.

Then he knew that there was a lack in his• life.
Ursan's words were its expression.

'Art thou in need of a friend ?'

He spoke abruptly, and sighed when he had
spoken. Alvo was silent.

'We may not meet again,' Ursan said. 'Tell me
thy story. It shall be safe with me.'

And Alvo, unable to resist the entreaty, whispered his story until the evening shadows fell.

Ursan listened attentively, but scarcely spoke till
it was ended. Then he said,—

'You wish to win the Fair Country for the Exiles?'

He smiled, and Alvo's heart choked him by its

beating ; but he made no answer, and none seemed to be expected.

That night he returned beneath the stars to the Helos' camp, reproaching himself silently and bitterly. He had been frank indeed to this enemy of his people, the wicked Maravel who was the tyrant of the Exiles ! And what could the old leader want with the unknown noble ?

' He will make me vain that he may make a fool of me,' thought Alvo.

Nevertheless it was not with reluctance that on the next day he returned to Ursan's tent. The Maravel had sent a message to the Helos that he must have the ' young leader ' in his camp.

From that time it was in the Maravel's camp that Alvo lived, fighting by his side in battle, sitting at his feet in Council, always distinguished by him with special favour, and every day trained by his experience. The powers of the young leader developed ; but his nature, long imprisoned, revenged itself by innumerable caprices, and his alternate fits of elation and depression perplexed the Rema who were his companions. His marvellous quickness, his childish eagerness, his reckless courage combined with dread of pain, made talk for the camp, and exercised upon it an indescribable mixture of fascination and repulsion. The Rema said he ' was made of the sea-foam,' and held him in less admiration than distrust. And yet it is true that beneath these varying humours there was little of real evil to be found.

That fact in itself was not the least remarkable; for evil was as life itself to Rema leaders, and the horrible licence which reigned within their camps was permitted and encouraged by their Maravel. It was strange that the youngest leader, with his restless, brilliant nature, should preserve himself from an universal taint; but various causes of nature and circumstance united from the beginning to protect him. Some safety Alvo owed to the clear sight of his ambition; still more to the remembrance of his sojourn with the priests; and yet more to the promises exacted from him by some noble women who once tended him when he was ill. He kept those promises, for, beneath its capricious surface, his nature had stuff which was tenacious. And, after all, the vision of the Fair Country held him captive: he did not dream of loving women, but of commanding men.

A dream that seemed vain! Alvo was still in Ursan's camp, when there came suddenly strange news of the Exiles—to the effect that, worn-out, oppressed, and in despair, they were abandoning the hope of the Alidrah. They would unite themselves with the long-haired Senas, and no longer assume to be sons of the Fair Country. A treaty to this effect was in course of preparation, when one morning Alvo burst in upon the Council.

He told Ursan afterwards that he was 'so mad with distress and pain he could not be certain what he said or did.' But, in fact, the speech that he poured out to the Exiles overwhelmed all opposition for the moment. Wild as it was, full of indefinite promises, its force and power awed them and kept them still. As men who are stunned, they looked at his burning eyes. Were the gods indeed speaking through the Estri's mouth ?

'I know it,' Alvo cried. 'I learned it on the mountains. The Great Spirit taught me there! We may return to our country ! The Gods will lead us. We need no other leader. I am not strong as other men ; I am weak in body and full of folly, and yet, if you were all to desert me, and I—I—I only were to fight, the Gods could still give us the Alidrah !'

He sat down, pale, trembling, and there was a long silence. And then one of the chiefs of the Senas rose.

'Ah! ah !' he said, 'are you going to believe in him, the slave Estri, who is so much afraid of pain ? '

He twisted his features, and some of the Exiles laughed. Alvo rose, quivering, with his eyes full of fire. Then the Sena cried out,—

'He—he—he is his mother's son!'

Alvo had been lately wounded, was excited beyond himself. He opened his lips, but no words came from them. In the midst of opposition he stood there, powerless. A deadly faintness overwhelmed him. He sat down and covered his face with his hands.

Then the consultation proceeded as before, and the Senas pressed the Exiles for an immediate decision: and the Exiles, hesitating, continually turned their eyes to the slim fingers clenched over a hidden face. Much pressed, and with many doubts, they almost agreed at last.

'But you will allow us some time before we sign the treaty?'

'How much time do you want?'

The last moment had come. Alvo rose, and spoke in a low, vibrating voice, which none present ever forgot.

'Give me two years, and I will win the Fair Country.'

Without waiting for an answer he strode from the council-room, and sought a dark wood, where he lay on the ground all night. The next morning he rode back to the camp, and before the sun had set had gained the name of Ursan's son. . . .

Doubtless at the moment the step seemed natural—and yet—Alvo, Alvo, thou didst not wait long for the assistance of the Gods!

Immediate results were successful. The community of Exiles received with frenzy the news of the alliance, but in spite of their fury they appeared to be content to delay the signing of the treaty for a while. And of those who were scattered amongst the mountain tribes, there were some who were roused to greater sympathy; for before many days had passed, there came to Alvo a band of men whom the rough mountain-life had trained. Many of these had the appearance of splendid soldiers, but the most notable was their chief—a tall, dark man who knelt down at the Estri's feet, and vowed to serve him in life and death. The name of this leader was Osmyn; and from that moment he became the Estri's right hand and counsellor.

More than a hundred came, and of these Alvo chose eighty-nine, because the number Ninety signified an unbroken bond. He had intended to be himself the ninetieth, and for some while resisted further offers; until, struck by the appearance of a handsome lad, he admitted him, and made him his shield-bearer. For this youth, who was the youngest of the band, he continued to display unusual affection. In this manner the 'Ninety' was formed; and Alvo gained a troop of soldiers devoted to his service.

And now—has not the young leader all that heart can wish? He is distinguished as a Maravel,

unrivalled in the use of weapons; he has earned
for himself wide-reaching name and fame; is the
favourite of Ursan, on his way to the Fair Country.
And yet the young face, with its worn outlines,
haunted eyes, conveys no expression less than
that of satisfaction—in spite of its continual flashes
into mirth, it remains the face of a troubled, careworn man. Ah, triumphant leader, Ursan's favourite,
even to you life has not been merciful!

' *There comes a time in the life of man* ' (this is a
legend of the Alidrah) ' *when the Nittrah* ' (fiends)
' *offer him a golden chain. If he accept it they drag
him by it to the heights, and their gift leads to
honour. But it is a chain.* '

Let us return to Alvo's tent.

.   .   .   .

Left to himself, Alvo continued to lean against
the pole, with his head drooping and his arms
hanging down, an attitude which would have
amazed his followers, and was only conceded to
his solitude. Yet, once assumed, it was not easily
to be changed; and he did not raise his head when
a familiar step approached. As the heavy curtain
dropped behind the new-comer he stood still,
struck by dismay and bewilderment.

' Estri, you are tired!'

' I have no time to be tired.'

The slightest complaint was unusual from Alvo.

For another moment his companion seemed bewildered, standing with his eyes fixed on his
master's face. Then, hastily advancing, he laid
hands on his master, lifted him from the ground
without any difficulty ; and, in this manner, bearing
him across the tent, laid him down on a mattress,
and piled cushions beneath his head. The action
was as rough as it was tender, but Alvo offered no
opposition ; for a moment he remained impassive,
then fell into peals of laughter.

' How darest thou, Osmyn ? ' he cried. ' Give
me my sword. How darest thou lay rebellious
hands upon thy leader ? '

' Estri, lie down, keep still,' muttered Osmyn,
in the reproving tones of a parent to a naughty
child.

' I never rest before noon.'

' That is folly, Estri. It would have been better
if thou hadst rested all the morning.'

' How could I rest ? I have been quarrelling
with Sidric. Osmyn, I have promised to teach
him his exercise.'

The face of Osmyn expressed his opinion.
Alvo clasped his hands as if he were pleading for
his life.

' Ah, Osmyn, be kind ! Do not be angry with
me. It is now only two days since I taught a
Rema.'

' I heard of that, Estri,' said Osmyn. ' I did not

expect it—even from thee. Estri, must thou direct every action in the camp?'

'I am its leader,' muttered Alvo, with a pout. But he added immediately, with his hands still more tightly clasped, 'Osmyn, forgive me, I will never teach another.'

The promise was not worthless, for it was one of the young leader's peculiar charms that, whenever it was possible, he always yielded to advice. But the stern, grave face watching him did not relent; for, except by silence, Osmyn never showed approval.

'Come and sit down by me,' Alvo cried out gaily, tossing together cushions with a skilful hand.

His counsellor sat down on them in the most upright manner, and turned a grave face to his master, who immediately replied,—

'Well, the news of the camp! Ah! there is something wrong. Go on. I can bear it.'

He made a child's grimace.

'Estri,' said Osmyn, speaking with reluctance, 'those two Gortona leaders have been drunk again.'

Alvo raised himself. He did not now look like a child.

'Didst thou remind them of my law?' he asked.

'I did, Estri; and they said they would not obey it.'

'Then tell them,' said Alvo, still more quietly, that leaders who disobey me will be hanged.'

'I did tell them, Estri; and they answered that the Gortona have no executioners.'

'Tell them,' said Alvo, 'that I will take the office on myself.'

Osmyn gave an involuntary glance to the supple fingers, loosely clasped. Alvo, meanwhile, appeared to be pondering.

'Bring them at some time to my tent to-morrow. Not to be hanged,' he cried, with peals of laughter, observing the bewilderment of his companion.

'No. I will talk to them, scold them, coax them, kiss them. I can often prevail.'

Osmyn again was silent.

'At what time shall they come?' Alvo asked. 'I shall be at work all day. And I have a Council to-night, and have promised to rise at dawn. Ah, they shall come to supper in my tent, *my* supper will be enough punishment for them! Next time they shall be hanged. And, now, tell me all the rest.'

He leaned his head on his hand, and turned up his face to hear.

Osmyn gave his report, and then Alvo spoke in turn, pouring out directions with inconceivable rapidity. No man but Osmyn could have listened to so many words, or remembered them if he had heard, or acted on them if he had remembered; but Alvo had learned to rely upon the follower who was habitually his right hand in the camp. Whilst he spoke his whole face was eager with the effort, but it relaxed into fatigue as soon as he had done.

'Osmyn, thou art tired,' he said, leaning on his cushions. 'I wish thou couldst rest.'

'That is folly, Estri,' said Osmyn. 'If I am tired it is of no consequence to the army. Thou art its leader, and shouldst take care of thyself.'

'Still rest,' murmured Alvo, in a caressing tone, with his face turned upwards towards his companion.

It is possible that Osmyn valued at its worth this anxiety from the man who had just loaded him with duties. But he loved his master.

'Ah, Estri,' he cried to him. 'Sleep now. Take a little rest. Be wise—for once.'

Alvo gave a swift, laughing glance; and then let his head sink, and his eyes droop luxuriously— the drooping eyes and smiles playing round his mouth giving his face an inexpressible look of fleeting beauty. The stern glance of Osmyn rested on it for a moment; his master could not see that expression of anxiety and sorrow.

'I give thee farewell, Estri,' he said in his grim voice.

'Live in health,' cried Alvo, with a merry intonation.

He had raised his head for the parting word and

smile, but he let it fall again immediately ; and as the curtain dropped behind his follower his breath came and went like that of a sleeping child.   Danger was near him—in the camp—beyond the camp— but still, for once he would rest—he would work when the heat was over.

Outside, the camp wakes from its noon-tide sleep; the watcher is still lingering in the ravine ; the men yawn and stretch themselves ; Osmyn goes about his duties ; in the intense light the woods look black and ragged ; a glare of blue sky is over all.

Now came still evening on, and twilight grey
Had in her sober livery all things clad.

In the twilight, in the evening, in the black and
dark night . . .

EVENING has come. The camp, which has been
noisy, is sinking now into its second, briefer silence ;
for there is always an interval of rest between sunset and the lighting of the torches. The shadow
of night has crept into the sky ; the first stars
shine ; the hills appear dark, gigantic ; a cold air
stirs the tent-curtains, all colours fade, and the
woods become indistinct.

'Evening is the time for meditation,' say the
sages of the Alidrah. On what matters does the
camp meditate during its interval of rest ?

The Rema, disdaining sleep, are lounging in
sullen groups, whispering to each other tales against
their leader. He has not been near them to play
the spy to-day ; he pretends to be ill, but he shall
not delay the Council ! They will soon disperse

to scatter these thoughts through the camp, where the Rema never fail to be ministers of evil.

For the moment, however, the camp is occupied, for on the exercise ground a slight stir is visible— a few torches are lit there, a dark group of men has gathered, and from all sides of the camp eyes are turned towards the place. The dark group of figures belong to Alvo's men, and others of his band are hastening to the spot. To all the Ninety this is the most pleasant time, the best-loved of the occupations of the day. The great Ilva—the largest of its giants—marshals them with his bronzed, uplifted arms.

Osmyn comes up, whispers a few words to Ilva, and goes on. The whisper spreads that Alvo will not leave his tent this evening. There is a groan of disappointment.

And now they are all arranged in martial order, grouped on the exercise ground, not far from their leader's tent. That tent is behind them on a rising ground, and at its side cluster a group of thorn-bushes. From these there looks out now a wild peering face, concealed by the leaves and the evening shadows. It is the man with the scar, and as he watches attentively, he keeps his hand always upon his breast. But he has no need to draw any hidden weapon, for his presence is not suspected by the soldiers.

They are too much occupied. Through the

whole extent of the camp there is a general stir of expectation ; dark faces peep out of tents, dark figures cluster ; even the Rema have for the present ceased to whisper. The soldiers on the exercise ground are motionless, with eyes fixed on Ilva, who swells with importance and delight. . . . And now there is silence. It is for this moment Ilva has waited. He lifts up his great dark arm towards the sky.

The stillness of the summer evening is broken by four voices, so absolutely together that the four sounds are one.

What is this ?—a wild, dreary chant, without melody or spirit—dull, monotonous ; was it for this the camp was waiting ? The low, deep voices are restrained almost to a murmur ; with perfect training they rise and fall together. This is a twilight prayer—the prayer to the Great Spirit, which is chanted at night in the homes of the Fair Country. The deep vibrations become slower and more sad, the echoes lower. The last thrill has died away. And now! the air is filled with a burst of melody, the seventy-two voices have joined in the Exiles' Song.

The Exiles' Song ! Indescribable is the very rush of sound, which without an effort fills the camp from end to end, sweeping beyond it to the silent woods, to the hill-sides which give back its echoes to the sky. Suffering is here, and triumph

the cry of hardship and oppression, almost lost in
the glory of the victory—for sorrow will be over,
the victory be won, the melody breaks into the
triumph of the chorus,—

> 'We will return to our country.'

A rush of sound comes at this instant from the
left, the Karngria to a man have all joined in the
chorus; for, words or no words, and meaning or
no meaning, it is impossible to hear without some
attempt to sing ! Their deep-toned voices peal
out like mighty bells—others, too, are assisting with
more or less of harmony—the Rema alone, clustered
in uneven groups, continue silent and scornful,
but attentive. This is the song without a birth,
without an author, the song that is the very voice
of banishment; wild, sorrowful, with outcries in
rudest rhythm, but possessed with triumph—We are
returning to our country ! Still firmer are the
voices, strong with coming victory, which lifts them
on the waves of sound towards the sky.

> Storm-clouds drift over us ;
> The waves of the sea are near us ;
>   Our enemies rejoice ;
> The demons laugh at us ;
> The night is dark and cold ;
>   The path is hard to find ;
> Yet we will return to our country
> Darkly frown the storm-clouds o'er us ;
>   Near are sorrow, want, and pain ;
> What care we what lies before us ?

We shall see our land again.
We will return to our country.
We will return—we will return—to our country.

The air is full of echoes, but the arm of Ilva sinks. The Song of the Exiles is over.

For an instant there is silence. The extraordinary excitement is succeeded by a sensation of lassitude, broken by the chattering voices of the Karngria, who are delighted with this evening ceremony. A few of the Rema have for the first time joined in the chorus, and this spreads discontent amongst the leaders of the Rema ; they sneer; Alvo's men become angry, and Ilva walks away in a rage. If Alvo were present he would be in the midst of the sullen ranks, and might compel even from the Rema an instant's graciousness ; but this ill-assorted camp, full of seething jealousies, will yield to no touch less potent than his own. The magic of the music was for an instant powerful ; but it is over—we have not yet gained our country !

Has *he* gained his desire, the man behind the bushes, lying now with his hands clenched, and his arms pressed upon his ears—or have the familiar chant and the unfamiliar chorus pierced him, as music has power to pierce ? As he raises his face at last, it is hard, and livid. On him also the music's influence has been present, and has passed. Still crawling, a noiseless though a wriggling shadow, he draws himself slowly towards Alvo's tent.

A glimmer shines from it, distinct in the night's darkness. He has travelled towards this moment —it has come.

The light between the folds is caused by Alvo's lamp. Alvo is alone in his tent, has been alone since Osmyn left him—an unusual circumstance, but he has felt the necessity of preparation for the approaching Council! During the afternoon he has prepared despatches, studied laws, perfected himself in languages and dialects, and written a long letter to a savage king in the hieroglyphics of the savages. The slow task is over, and he can allow himself some rest before evening brings the torches and the Council; but his face darkens when, as he lifts his head, he catches the sounds of anger from the camp.

'Never an instant's peace by day or night! How can I rest in such a camp as this?'

Ah, how can he rest—condemned by Ursan's order to remain stationary instead of leading his troops to battle, to struggle day by day with the contentions of those troops, waiting always for the money which the Maravel delays? A hard look is in Alvo's face, a strange glitter in his eyes, through his clenched teeth his breath comes angrily; and then his face softens and his lips relax, as with the touch of old remembrance.

'He has never refused me anything that I asked him face to face.'

A wild idea crosses his mind. What if he left his camp this night, and riding day and night to the other camp by the Tordrade, should fling himself on his knees before the Maravel of the Rema, and implore his father to deal with him openly? For one moment his eyes are lit with sudden hope; but for a moment only, as the next thought recalls his camp—the seething camp, whose perpetual rebellions refuse to be curbed by any other hand. No, he must wait—he and his men must wait for some final decision from the old Maravel. And, meanwhile, the senses of Alvo are too keen for him to be unconscious of approaching danger. Only this morning he has sent a bitter message—a message which may draw the lightning down at last!

'The Leopard sends to me his most gracious words—the Leopard is always at his softest when he is about to spring. He knows that the Rema conspire, that the mountain-tribes are insolent, that this delay gives time for preparation in the Alidrah —it is for these reasons that he leaves me here, powerless, that every hope may decay until he has punished me enough! And then he writes to me words as if he loved me!' but once more the lines of Alvo's face relax. 'He has never refused me any-thing that I asked him face to face.'

Ah, what is the use of fears? he will let himself dream for a while, and that he may dream he presses his palms against his ears—he is in the tent

of the Maravel of the Rema, sitting at his feet
during a midnight council—no, he is upon a lonely
mountain-path with only yellow-haired Ivlon at
his side, the Fair Country is won, and he has given
up his power that at last, at last he may be able to
please himself—he is lying beneath apple-boughs,
and close to him stands a slender maiden, looking
down with serious eyes. His palms press more
closely upon the delicate ears which even in sleep
can be keen to the slightest sound. They are
closed from duty, or else they might have warned
him of the presence of an intruder in his tent. For
already between the outer and inner curtains stands
the watcher with his hand on the weapon at his
breast. The last moment has come, in another
instant he will be face to face with the terror of the
Alidrah.

'Quick—quick!' whispers a voice at the watcher's
heart. 'Do not wait—do not stay to think—it will
be over in a moment.' With a noiseless movement
he draws the weapon from his breast. 'Quick—
quick,' cries the voice; 'if you delay it will be too late.'

His hand is on the curtain. There is no sound
to be heard. Yes, there is the sound of a man's
quiet breathing. His face becomes ghastly. He
feels the edge of the weapon. His lips sneer—
'And now, look to yourself, young leader.'

He moves the curtain. He is moving in a dream.
He can see the still lamp-light, and the crouching

figure. His weapon is in his hand : he need not strike more than once. Now ! . . . A strong grasp seizes him, and he is dragged back from the tent.

'Aha! Who are you who come to the tent of our little leader? I was watching you—I, Sidric! I knew your ugly face. So you think we do not take care of him, our little leader?'

Alvo gets up hastily, and overturns the lamp. The cries of Sidric summon others to his assistance. For, stunned during the first instant, and deprived during that instant of his weapon, the would-be murderer is now fighting for his life. And so active is he that the whole strength of the giant is barely sufficient to detain him in his grasp.

But the camp has been alarmed. Men are rushing to the spot. There is a confused clamour of voices and footsteps. Torches are lit hastily, questions pour from every side, there is a general sensation of terror and insecurity. What has happened? Is the Estri hurt? Where is the man? Where is the Estri? The questions rush upon each other. From the distance come the voices of sentinels, imploring to be told what has occurred. Meanwhile, one torch after another is lit, until the camp, so dark before, appears in a blaze of light.

And the murderer?

It is a wonder that he is alive, for he has been struggling against a multitude ; but, beaten down,

trodden on continually, he has risen, as with a
demon's strength, to strive again.   At last, however, he has been raised by many hands from the
ground, and has been bound, eyes, hands and feet,
and left in the strong grasp of Osmyn until his
doom shall be pronounced.   To him the struggle
has been the bewilderment of fever ; it has been a
clamour of voices, the oppression of a nightmare ;
and now, wounded, panting, almost unconscious, he
leans against Osmyn that he may rest before his
doom.   When the last moment comes, and it cannot be long delayed, to what sort of country will
this man return ?

He feels no remorse, no fear, no disappointment,
only one wish, craving as the thirst of the dying.
If he could look for an instant on the terror of the
Alidrah, if he could see him, or even hear his voice!
He listens eagerly, but in the multitude of sounds
the tones of the leader are not to be distinguished.
And now and then even these sounds become in-
distinct, and he would fall if he did not cling to
Osmyn.   The grasp of Osmyn is not rough like
that of others, but it is stern, there is no pity in it.

And now he has been taken from Osmyn, and
they are dragging him away.   The air of the night
is cold to his wounded shoulders.   They will kill
him now, and then he will never see. . . . They
are standing still.   What will they do with him ?

'Estri,' cries an eager voice, ' turn round and look.'

A sudden and complete silence falls upon the camp. Through that silence the captive hears a voice.

'He is young.'

The words, half-surprised, half-pitying, have a strange effect on the man of whom they are spoken. He puts out his bound hands wildly, as if he would grasp the speaker, then everything sinks. . . .

'He faints,' Alvo says. 'Take him to my tent and revive him, for I must speak with him before he dies.'

He is carried away.

And now Alvo stands before his tent, looking down upon multitudes. The last instants have been difficult, for he has been embraced, congratulated, belaboured with questions, grasped by many hands. It seems impossible for his soldiers to believe in his safety until they have subjected him to treatment rough enough to endanger it. He has rescued himself at last from those clinging arms, and now stands on the slope before his tent that all may see him. A man behind him holds a torch whose glow is lurid. Alvo appears somewhat pale and agitated.

In the camp dark suspicions are floating.

'I do not like this attempt,' whispers the oldest commander of the Rema to the young Rema whom we know. 'There are many here who hate him; I trust—none of our men—'

'If I could believe as much of any one of mine,
I would kill him with my own hands.'

Alvo looks down on the multitude. Perhaps
these suspicions have a voice for him as well. His
face is unusually thoughtful and absorbed. He has
taken a gold charm from his breast, and presses it.

'So thou art not killed yet, Estri,' cries the jovial,
delighted Ilva.

Alvo answers,—

'It was not time.

His own words sound ominous. He must shake
off this black mood, it is the moment for gaiety.
No man is more used to control his moods than
Alvo; with the thought comes the smile that
floods his dark eyes with light. The young
Karngri, standing below, looks at him with admiration. In spite of himself he is attracted by
his leader.

'Art thou certain thou art not hurt, Maravel?'
he asks.

Alvo turns to him a quick, penetrating glance.
It rests on the open face with relief.

'Ah, Prince,' says Alvo softly, in the language of
the Karngria, 'I had not a moment in which to
speak to thee this morning. We must know more
of each other.'

The Karngri blushes with satisfaction, but his
friend's voice is at his ear.

'I told thee!'

Alvo's ears are keen for whispers.

'What didst thou tell him?'

The Rema blushes in his turn. But he has a spice of his nation's insolence.

'Maravel, I told him that thou wouldst speak to him in the Karngri language.'

Alvo bites his lips, but only says as he turns away,—

'Until thou canst whisper lower, thou wilt not make a conspirator.'

'After all,' mutters the Karngri, 'his face is wonderful.'

'Bah!' replies the other, 'he is a man with a woman's tricks.'

These also turn away, but the multitude still lingers. Alvo talks apart with Osmyn.

'The man is in my tent?'

'Yes, Estri.'

'Poor wretch, he must die before the morning. Tell the soldiers, and send them away. I am weary of the noise.'

But although Alvo is weary of the noise he goes round among the troops, dispensing the gracious words that are valuable from a leader. Even now, however (his graciousness being rarely perfect), there is a passage-at-arms between him and the leader of the Rema.

'We must thank the Akbare,' cries the honest, delighted Ilva.

'Truly,' answers the old chief of the Rema, 'since they have preserved so wise a leader. Yet the sages say life is more dangerous than death.'

'They mean when a man has secret enemies,' murmurs Alvo. 'But I have so many friends.'

He glances at the whispering groups of Rema, and moves away.

In a few minutes he is standing before his tent, alone with Sidric. Beneath them are sounds of voices from the camp; but here, under the great hills, all is silence.

'Estri, the Rema did not like your words.'

'I regret them,' sighs Alvo. 'I speak too hastily. And I have never even thanked you, my faithful Sidric.'

'You never need, Estri. Thank the gods. They have saved you for us.'

Alvo looks at him with sadness in his glance.

'I thank the gods, Sidric. Ah, I hope I shall not live to make you all wish that I had died! Go and sleep now, Sidric. Come to my tent at dawn.'

And they separate.

Meanwhile, Olbri had been waiting in Alvo's tent, bound to the post on which the leader had leaned that morning. It was evident that he had reached the crisis of his fate. What were his feelings?

He had failed to commit a murder, he knew himself about to die, and it might be supposed that he would be oppressed. But, in truth, he was not, he was possessed with the strangest ease, almost surprised at his own placidity. Death could not be worse than life; and now that he had failed in his intention, he was not sure that he would have been glad to have succeeded. At last —*at last*—he was beneath even the reach of pain.

'I will leave it to the birds to find something good in me.'

Alvo entered.

Olbri had heard his voice outside, although he was not able to distinguish words. Already he knew it—rapid, low, distinct, with a vibration like the ring of metal. He had wished to see the young leader, and though that wish itself was dull, it yet made him turn his head towards the entrance. But the tent was dark, and he could distinguish nothing. Alvo passed by him and raised the fallen lamp.

Seated on his mattress, he trimmed it, as if he had no other thought, although he must have been aware of the presence of the prisoner. Olbri could not but look down on the stooping figure, upon the fingers playing with the flame.

'They move well and quickly,' he thought, with a sensation of interest unworthy of a man beneath the reach of pain.

But now Alvo rose, hung the lamp upon a hook, and turned quietly towards the prisoner. So for the first time they stood face to face—the son of the sorcerer and the sorcerer.

The first glance tells little.   Alvo saw a scar ;
Olbri a face in which were gleaming eyes.   Something scornful, inquiring, in the glance of those
dark eyes, produced a faint feeling of opposition
in his breast.

'He means to question me, but I will tell him
nothing.   I will not say another word until I die.
My life, at any rate, has made silence easy.   I will
die even more silently than I have lived.'

Still Alvo did not speak.

'So this is the wizard,' Olbri thought, 'a man
whose forehead is lost in maiden's curls.   I need
not have come so far to look at him, we have
pretty fops even in the Fair Country. . . . But this
one is clever . . .' he began to feel uneasy beneath
the magnetism of the leader's eyes.

'Art thou hurt ?' asked Alvo gently.

He had already become aware that this man
with the horrible scar was no common criminal.
There was a mixture of disdain and compassion
in his tone ; Olbri's eyes resented the scorn, and
flung the compassion away.   He pushed his face
forward insolently, remembering his hideous scar.
Alvo smiled slightly, without drawing back.

'A strange mark,' he said, looking at it criti-
cally ; and, putting out two careless fingers, he
drew them lightly down the scar.

The touch was successful, Olbri could not preserve composure ; angry blood rushed to his fore-

head, tears of humiliation to his eyes. Alvo looked
at him curiously, and then said,—

'Forgive me.'

He already regretted his experiment. Olbri,
ashamed, resolute, muttered to himself,—

'He may make me weep, but he shall not make
me speak.'

The lamp shone on the two faces, the leader
and the criminal, as different as if they had been
some result of contrast.

Alvo had determined that he would not leave
this man until he had forced from him an answer
he required.

Olbri stood before him, his hands bound behind his back, his clothes almost torn away from
breast and shoulders, his face drawn, distorted, his
hair long and tangled, the brutal aspect of the detected murderer. No easy task would it be to
overcome him, but the young leader was used to
dubious battles. His voice, when he broke the
silence, had the sound of a resolve, but it retained
even more than its usual gentleness.

'You must die before the morning . . . the
soldiers will have told you . . . but first there are
some questions that I wish you to answer. It will
not injure you to answer them. . . . I wish to
save you from torture, if possible.'

Alvo looked, and saw that this gentle hint of
torture had at once steeled the prisoner's nerves;

but he was not discouraged; on the contrary, he was relieved. He preferred to deal with a man who was not a coward. He began his questions, but he asked them carelessly, as if he were indifferent whether he were answered.

'Art thou from the Alidrah?'

He waited a moment, then went on, scarcely pausing between each question that he asked.

'Thy name? Thy rank? For what reason didst thou wish to kill me? How wert thou able to enter the camp?'

He paused; and Olbri, not understanding his intention, turned away his face as if the bright eyes could *force* answers. This time Alvo waited longer and when he spoke it was evident that he spoke with earnestness.

'Thou dost not answer? Well, it may be that thou art right. These questions concern only thyself . . . But I have one more to ask.'

His face seemed to become hard and dark, but there was a doubtful light upon it. The change in his voice, however, was not to be mistaken.

'Did any one in my camp know of thy purpose —any one? If thou sayest that all were ignorant I can believe thee. If thou art silent I shall know whom to suspect. Now! Speak or be silent.'

Olbri was silent.

Thou dost not speak,' muttered Alvo. 'Remember, this is a matter of life or death to others.

Did others know? I need not ask thee any names. *They did know!* Thou dost not deny it?'

Olbri was silent as before.

Silent! but he felt as if every pulse were beating with the fierce words in which throbbed a lifetime's bitterness.

'Thy father suffered, being innocent—thou hast suffered, innocent—the innocent may now suffer for thee. *And they shall suffer,*' muttered Olbri.

Alvo fixed a keen gaze on his unchanging face; and then turned away, as if he were satisfied.

'It is so! I knew it!' he said, below his breath, and this time it was beyond doubt that he was changed—that his eyes were contracted, dark, and that his face had lost its beauty.

'Ye think the young leader so gentle,' said the oldest Rema chief. 'I tell you he has it in him to be cruel like other men.'

Olbri, watching closely, became aware of the vibration which, for an instant, shook him from head to foot.

'Aha!' he said to himself, 'I have touched the wizard after all!'

But Alvo only turned quietly away, and trimmed the lamp.

When he returned his face showed no agitation; the blood had come back to his lips, and his eyes looked bright and gentle.

'I will ask thee no more,' he said to Olbri,

speaking softly, 'and I will not torture thee for the sake of information. When the soldiers return in a few minutes thou must die. But I will give thee no pain that is not necessary.'

Olbri scanned him in vain for any sign of his late emotion. Finding none, he said to himself, ' He is not a coward.'

Alvo, meanwhile, sat down once more on his mattress, and began to repair an old sword belt daintily.

The minutes passed. Olbri still felt no fear—remorse; he was resting, at ease, pleased by the approach of death, even soothed by the dull throb which continued in his brain ;

'Your father suffered, being innocent — you suffered, innocent.' He did not move his face, or the arms bound behind his back ; he stood against the post, looking down on his companion. The little interest which his life retained could be found at that instant in that companion's face.

'So, I have seen the wizard—I have thrown a fire-brand in his camp—and now I shall die, and forget the pain of life.' And still the dull throb continued ceaselessly,—

'Your father suffered, being innocent — you suffered, innocent.'

Old memories restored him to the time when he had fever, when his head rested upon his father's shoulder—to that other moment when, in an impulse of reparation, the young nobleman had piled

the flowers upon his breast. But his father and
Ascar were faint like distant shadows; he knew
that he was unworthy of their love. And now
Alvo raised his head, and said in his low, clear
voice :

'I will call the soldiers.'

As he spoke he held out the sword-belt, and his
eyes rested on his work with youthful satisfaction.
Then he glanced suddenly, with some shame, at
the captive; and as their eyes met Olbri smiled
irresistibly. Perhaps the smile relieved the young
leader; for, rising immediately, he touched the
captive's arm, murmured, 'You are brave,' and left
the tent. He did not know what a tumult of reaction his three words had roused in his companion's breast.   •

Soldiers were round him—they were unbinding
him—he struggled to speak, as one striving with a
nightmare.

'Estri—Estri—' he gasped. And then, as a
dream changes, the men were gone—he and Alvo
were alone.

'What is it?' asked Alvo, in his sternest voice.
'Say what thou wilt, but I cannot promise thee
thy life.'

Olbri tried to speak, but his white lips would
only tremble; he seemed to have lost the power of
pronouncing words. Then Alvo brought water,
almost impatiently, and wetted his forehead and

lips. His touch had no pity, but it had gentleness, and Olbri felt a certain pleasure in the contact.

'What is it?' asked Alvo. 'Thou hast not more than an instant.'

Olbri gathered his strength.

'Estri, I have lied to thee.'

'Thou hast not even spoken.'

'I have deceived thee without speaking. Estri, I know no man in thy camp. The innocent shall not suffer for me.'

Alvo looked at him with amazement.

'How can I believe thee?'

'I entreat thee to believe me. I would not have any man's blood upon my head. I come from the Fair Country. I travelled over the plain alone. I came in with the rabble this morning, and hid all day in the ravine. No man knew of my purpose, no man but myself. I entreat thee, believe me.'

'Why didst thou not speak before?'

'Because I wished that the innocent should suffer.'

'Thou art worse than a coward!'

Olbri was silent.

'Tell me why thou wouldst kill me.'

'Estri,' said Olbri, wearily, 'call the soldiers. Let me die at once.'

'Answer me first.'

Olbri looked blankly round the tent, at the lamp, the shadows, the tired face of Alvo. Why

had he wished to kill him? The words came in a
trembling voice.

'Because they banished me.'

Alvo had not expected the answer. He started,
and for one instant surveyed the prisoner. His
words were abrupt.

'Thou hast been branded?'

'Yes, Estri,' muttered Olbri.

'And for what reason?'

'They called me a coward, but I am not one—
I am not.'

Alvo smiled disdainfully.

'He who crawls to men's tents by night—'

'They kill wild beasts at night.'

The young leader laughed.

'After all, thou hast real courage. I am glad.
That will make it an easier matter for thee to die.'

He came close to Olbri, and laid a hand upon
his arm. Something in the prisoner had attracted
him.

'Ah! dost thou know,' he murmured, in an outburst of confidence, 'I would not be quite sorry if
I changed with thee, and lost my tired head, and
the Council, and all the burden of the camp. The
moon shines to-night!'

The strange words were sincere enough; they
had the fascination of sincerity. A sudden flood
rushed over Olbri. In that instant it was impossible not to express his penitence.

'Estri,' he cried, 'I was wrong—I am a sinner. Thou art too generous to me who have tried to murder thee. I am worse than an animal, but I was mad—in despair. They killed my father by their cruelty, they punished me when I had done no wrong, they drove me away from my home and my father's grave. I had no home, no country. Estri, it is a hard lot to have no country.'

He spoke the words as they came, without pausing to consider. He had no thought of making the least appeal for mercy. But if he had searched through all the words he knew, he could have found none more fitted to reach the heart of the young leader. The face of Alvo changed, it appeared that he was moved.

'Thou art right,' he said in a low voice, as if he were speaking to himself; 'it is a hard lot to have no country.'

Without looking again at Olbri he paced up and down the tent. Suddenly he stopped, and then turned and went out. Olbri looked after him in some surprise, but he was tired . . . it was all a dream . . . he fell back to unconsciousness.

And Alvo was standing with Osmyn upon the deserted exercise - ground, looking down on the darkness, the bright lights of the camp. The sky was covered with drifting, fleecy clouds, through which the moon sent some gleams of shivering light.

'Osmyn—Osmyn, why may I not pardon him?'

'Because he deserves to die.'

'Do we not all deserve to die?'

'That is folly, Estri. Of course thou wilt have thy way. I can only tell thee what the soldiers already say. They say that the man must be a friend of the Rema.'

'They may say so.'

'And the Rema say that if he were one of them—'

'They tell the truth. I should certainly not spare a Rema. It would be an advantage to the world to have one Rema less in it.'

'Estri, dost thou remember that the Rema may be listening?'

'Ah, they may,' cried Alvo. 'I thank thee for reminding me. I will go and eat supper with my murderer.'

He turned away, laughing; and Osmyn looked after him with a dark face, crushing his heel against the ground. But, the moment's anger over, he followed his master at a distance, determined to watch by the young leader's tent. He would lose his supper, and his only time for leisure, but these were small losses for his master's sake.

The hills frown, unfathomable darkness fills the valleys; the camp is still silent in spite of its gleams of light; somewhere in the distance a soldier is bawling to the sky,—

'We will return to our country.'

Tender is the night,
And haply the Queen-Moon is on her throne . . .
But here there is no light,
Save what from heaven is with the breezes blown.

The Queen-Moon rises. She sweeps away the clouds; and, riding the sky, pours her light on Alvo's camp. Further away that light falls upon woods and rivers; on the lonely paths trodden by some captives, whom we know; on the meadows and groves of the beautiful Alidrah; on the glistening Tordrade, and the revels of Ursan's men. The Queen-Moon has the same gift; she rides the sky, and pours down her cold light from her silver throne. It is to that weird light, beneath that silent sky, that Olbri must go out to begin his life again.

A night of wonders! Olbri had been roused from stupor by the soldiers who told him that they came to set him free, and who laughed at him when he implored that he might die. He was unbound; his wounds were bandaged, and he was provided with food and clothes, and told that at midnight he must leave the camp; whilst, with the earnestness of a last entreaty, he only asked to see and speak with Alvo. Olbri could not have told why he proffered this request; it was not with any wish to express his gratitude, some strange attraction had laid hold of him.

And then Alvo returned; and Olbri could not speak, though Alvo had smiled, and told him he might rest; and then, with his ordinary reckless courage, had thrown himself down upon the ground to write. He paid not the least further heed to his companion; and Olbri, standing, looked down on him and thought.

What should he do with his life? He must again begin to live, and that is a hard task when a life has failed. His father was dead; and though Ascar might be alive, he had promised not to bring the 'curse of the banished' on his friend. Must he still fight alone? He was weary of the struggle, tired of the opposing eyes of multitudes; and yet when his mind turned to the thought of solitude, he was only able to recall its bitterness. With despairing eyes, and yet with some interest, his glance now fell upon his companion. In after days he would be able to remember that he had looked, as in a dream, on the terror of the Alidrah.

'Dark hair, with a nut-brown tint, kept closely cut, but allowed to lie in small, fine rings on his forehead. . . . Ah! I remember that he has a scar;

he has the vanity to wish to hide it. . . . Dainty
black eyebrows (one is injured by the scar) and
eyelashes that curl as if they were a girl's . . . and
I have seen his eyes, brown eyes with dark grey
rims, as clear and deep as if they were wells of light.
Ah! why did the gods condemn that pretty face
to go into the hard life of battles and be spoiled?
the hard life!—'

Alvo threw back his head with a petulant, weary
motion, raising his arms and letting his tablets fall.
His lips pouted, his eyes sought those of Olbri with
a childish, tired expression . . . and Olbri flung
himself at the young leader's feet.   There had been
nothing to prepare his companion for the movement, which was not less unexpected by himself.

'Estri, take me with thee, take me to the
Alidrah!'

For one moment Alvo was silent from surprise.

'Rise,' he said then, 'thou dost not know what
thou askest.'

'Take me to the Alidrah,' entreated Olbri.

'I may never reach it.'

The young leader's voice was hoarse.   But Olbri
clung to his knees in an agony.

'At least I shall be near thee.'

Alvo did not smile.   He looked gravely down
on his companion.

'Rise,' he said; 'sit down, do not vex thyself.   I
will help thee if I can.'

He began to pace his tent. Olbri, still trembling, sat down upon the ground. Alvo walked up and down, with his hands behind his back.

The appeal had distressed more than it had astonished him, for it was not the first time he had seen a man at his feet, and it was impossible for him to be ignorant of the spell which he exercised so easily. But, if he had once felt a youthful pleasure in such magic, in these darker days, oppressed even by his men's devotion, he was perpetually haunted by a whisper, 'Never tempt any man *now* to follow thee.' The whisper recurred to him ; but his brain, always keen and subtle, replied that this man at least had not been tempted, and that it was written on the scarred, wasted face that its owner would prove no ordinary follower. For a moment he wavered, but the indecision passed ; he could not now venture on any difficulty. Yet he felt a pang, for no ordinary attraction drew him to this man who had tried to murder him. He came close to Olbri, who was still seated on the ground.

'Listen,' he said, 'I will speak to thee honestly. It is in my power to keep thee in my camp, in spite of the jealousy both of my soldiers and the Rema. But what wilt thou gain? Thy country is thy home, thy friends.'

'I have no friends,' said Olbri.

'Then at least thy memories. Wilt thou be con-

tent to come with an army there? I can fight for
a land which I have never known.'

Olbri pondered.

'I have Ascar. I have my father's grave . . .
But how else can I reach them? There is nothing
left for me in life.'

'Nothing but me—the wild beast?' cried Alvo,
laughing. 'No, thou art wrong, there is one other
way. The Avra Nira are raising an army. They
take any men who come. They ask no questions
concerning their history. Go to them, and tell them
that you come from Alvo's camp. They will accept
thee gladly for the sake of information. Choose!'

Alvo raised his tablets, and began again to write,
leaning against the pole, and glancing down on
Olbri; who sat with blank eyes and hesitating lips,
as if he were lost in some uncertain dream. Ah!
he could willingly have followed the young leader!
but then Ascar—Ered—*that other*—his dead father
—all these dead, living hands which had once
touched him kindly were stretched out against him
now as barriers. And the young leader, however
beautiful, generous, was bringing the Rema to the
Fair Country! Yet he hesitated, and it was only
with reluctance that he rose slowly, sadly, to his feet.

'Hast thou decided?'

'Yes, Estri.'

Olbri looked down on the ground. Alvo came
close to him, and touched his arm.

'We shall meet in battle. I long to fight again! And now come and have supper with me before the Council.'

An enchanted supper!

Side by side with the young leader, Olbri sat down on cushions on the ground, before the simple food which Alvo's own hands had prepared, for he was accustomed to wait upon himself. Olbri was tired; he could feel now that he had been bruised; a strange, dreaming atmosphere seemed to enfold his senses, and there were moments when it was impossible for him to believe that he was indeed close to the terror of the Fair Country. The two men ate in silence; the captive possessed with craving hunger, but Alvo scarcely touching the food that was before him—scarcely even drinking, although at intervals he placed his dry lips on the mouth of the jar of water. He appeared to be feverish, absorbed in thought; all at once, flinging off the Council, he turned suddenly to his companion.

'Thou lookest earnestly at me. What dost thou want?'

'I wanted—to remember thy face.'

'Look at it again.'

Olbri did look, but this time he saw nothing, for the young leader met his eyes with his own penetrating glance.

'I would forget the Council,' Alvo murmured.
'Talk to me.'

And the enchanted meal was succeeded by an
enchanted conversation !

The men sat on the ground.   The lamp flickered
above their heads ; from without came the distant
murmur of the camp.   Olbri was still in a dream,
but his companion's eyes demanded speech, and he
could not but answer to their sympathy.   The two
men—so different !—were yet near each other ; for
one moment at least their fates had touched.

'There is little to tell, Estri,' Olbri said in a hard
voice, whilst his face became rigid, and his pale
eyes fixed.   'For years of my life I was left entirely
alone.   I was still a boy when my father—went
into Silence.'

He paused.

'My father was learned—he knew the herbs and
stars—and the neighbours hated him, they accused
him of being a wizard.   They ill-treated him ; they
left him to die alone—alone, without food—there
was no food near him when I found him—I found
his dead body lying on the ground—I knew then
what men were—' He shivered at the remembrance.

'And what didst thou then ?' whispered Alvo,
anxious to draw him from his thoughts, for Olbri
had twisted his fingers as if he were in mortal
pain.   It was only with an effort that he roused
himself.

'I—I learned the herbs and stars—one can learn many things from them—my father used to say that they are wise and gentle. And I hunted—'

'I once loved hunting,' Alvo cried.

'I hunted to live, Estri; I killed the animals for their skins. But I was sorry for the animals; I would rather have killed men.'

'Wise and gentle as the herbs and stars,' whispered Alvo, with a smile.

'Estri, if men had killed your father—'

'They killed my mother.'

There was silence.

'I know not what comes after life;' said Olbri, 'but life itself is a hard thing—hard to me.'

Alvo looked at him, and his voice sank low.

'Thou canst scarcely have had a harder life than mine.'

For one instant Olbri was silent, then he cried,—

'Estri, thy face is not scarred.'

But Alvo laughed, and pushed back the dark rings from his forehead, The movement revealed that on his left hand too there was a scar.

'Yes, Estri,' said Olbri, bitterly; 'and when men see those marks they say: "Ah, the brave leader, these are tokens of his battles!" not: "This fellow has a disease, let us keep away from him;" or, "Here is a wretch who has been branded, and has tried in vain to remove the brand."'

'Why did they brand thee?'

'They said I was a coward. Estri, thou wilt not believe me, but I was not one, I was not.'

Alvo looked at him with his piercing glance.

'I believe thee,' he murmured.

Tears rose to Olbri's eyes.

'See, now,' said Alvo kindly, 'thou art foolish! What should it matter to thee whether I believe or not? A leader is always a coward; if he retreats it is the cowardice of terror; if he advances it is the cowardice of despair. No—no—it is to our own hearts we must look.

'And too often,' he muttered, 'we find ourselves cowards there.'

There was an instant's silence.

'How did'st thou remove the brand?'

'I burned my face with the vera loni' (*burning juice*).

'That must have been a painful remedy.'

'It was,' said Olbri, laughing at the remembrance. 'I howled, for I was in a wood, and there were none to hear. I did not mean to distort my face so much—I was vexed when I saw it, but the brand was gone.

'Again!' cried Alvo. 'What was the brand to thee?'

'It was enough, Estri, to drive me from my senses.'

'Perhaps,' murmured Olbri, with a glance at his

companion, 'thou wouldst care more for the disfigurement.'

'I should,' replied Alvo, simply. 'I should let my face alone, and leave it to my battles to remove the brand. But then I know that I am always called a coward. The voices of others do not trouble me.'

'That is my weakness, Estri, but I cannot cure it, although I have had ill words round me from my childhood. Ah, how I have longed for kindness! My father used to say, "More men go hungry for kindness than for bread." And then, if one keeps alone, there are thoughts like demons—'

Alvo made a sign of assent. He added quickly,—

'Why didst thou not study?'

'I was always angry, like a fool; and he who is angry cannot learn the herbs and stars. And then I would be seized with a desire to hunt, and would rush out into the free air and the dew. And so I could learn nothing.'

'Yes; nothing,' Alvo muttered. 'That is not the way in which any work is done. The gods demand a whole life—' his face became dark. The next words scarcely stirred his lips, 'Yet the gods are good.' There were others to which he would give no utterance. 'In spite of all I will win the Fair Country.'

Feeling that his hand clenched, he turned round

to Olbri with a gay, careless look that might have been a child's.

'We must part directly. It is almost time for the Council. Is there any boon I can grant thee?'

'Estri, I could ask it on my knees. I have one friend—one—who has been good and generous. His name is Ascar. He is a captive of the Rema. I have been branded, and might bring a curse on him. But I have given jewels to his bride. She may come to thee—'

'I will try to help him.'

'And—thou wilt spare her? She is beautiful.'

'A woman is safe in my camp,' Alvo answered with steady eyes. 'Art thou ready to leave me now? Where wilt thou go?'

'To the Avra Nira.'

'Art thou in want of food?'

'I left my bow and arrows outside the camp. May I have my knife?'

'It shall be given back to thee. Is it poisoned?' Olbri made a sign of assent.

'Thou art wrong,' said Alvo, speaking seriously. 'A man who can strike straight is in no need of poison. That is not warfare.'

'It is a just reproof. But I thought that if I struck a man his face might become like mine.'

Alvo raised his eyebrows.

'Estri, I have been wrong. I will not ask for my knife. I will begin my life again.'

' Learn the will of the gods.'

' I know so little of the gods. (Does *he* know much ?' thought Olbri). ' But I will try.'

' And, at least,' said Alvo, looking at him with a smile, ' thou wilt know that one man in the great world believes in thee.'

Olbri tried to speak, but his eyes became dim with tears. And now Osmyn and Ilva entered the tent side by side.

The two soldiers looked disdainfully at the captive, but Ilva's disdain was soon lost in the joy of Alvo's presence. Osmyn stood apart, more dark and grim than usual, because he knew that his master had despised his counsel. As for Alvo, he whispered and laughed with the giant Ilva, whilst Olbri watched him, almost with perplexity.

' Does he indeed bewitch men ? Am I bewitched ? He is beautiful, but he is not like Ascar —whom I love.'

Alvo came near him.

' Ilva will take thee out of the camp. We shall meet in battle.'

He laid a kind touch on Olbri's arm. Mechanically Olbri followed Ilva's steps. They had almost reached the curtain of the tent when suddenly he turned back, threw himself down upon his knees, and grasping the young leader's hands, covered them with kisses.

' If I could meet thee again, Estri !'

Olbri's voice was choked with tears.

'We shall meet in battle,' said Alvo. 'Live in health.'

'Come, then,' muttered Ilva in a gruff, kindly voice. Ilva was touched by the scene, but Osmyn looked more grim than ever.

Olbri rose from his knees, and followed Ilva into the camp, into the starlit darkness, and began his life again. . . .

Meanwhile the Council assembled. Alvo kept Osmyn close to him, with an inward hope that he would be edified.

Perhaps Osmyn *was* edified. It had happened, from various causes that he had not before been present at a Council ; and, long accustomed as he was to his master's manners, he could not but wonder at them anew on this occasion. Alvo received his guests, who for the most part were grey-headed, with the most becoming deference, the most shy humility ; his words of greeting being few, grave, and simple, never sinking below the dignity of the occasion. It was with the same manner of attention and respect that he listened to their opinions when the Council had begun. The Rema, always ready to find some fault with him, could have told that he was not always so modest at a Council.

Most of them remembered very different meetings when they had squatted on the ground round their old Maravel; whilst Alvo leaned on Ursan's knee, impatient, eager, only restrained by the old hand that rested on his shoulder. Those meetings were also in the young leader's mind; he had once taken pleasure in the Councils of the Maravel.

Now he sat at the head of his own, perched on a stool, whose height was supposed to add to his dignity; whilst Osmyn stood behind him in grim, disapproving silence, and below him were the dark faces of the oldest leaders in his camp. There were the Rema, sharp, contemptuous; the Kroni, whose features might have been carved in wood; the Karngria, with their long beards falling on their breasts, each with a red spot on the right hand which had shed blood. It was strange to turn from these men to the beauty of the leader; he seemed to be ill-fitted to control them all.

Yet Alvo understood his business. In spite of his youthfulness, the curls on his forehead, the fever in his cheeks, the drooping, black eyelashes that veiled his eyes, he was always able to make his position felt. The look of wonder by which he replied to insolence; the little compliments by which he soothed and pleased; the voice which, however low, was not without vibrating power—these gifts had their own subduing influence. He rarely gave his opinion, and when he did so his voice trembled, an effect which the Rema noted as hypocrisy—though it was rather due to the peculiar sensitiveness which kept him always conscious that he was in the midst of enemies. The involuntary tremor did not affect his words, which never failed to be deserving of attention.

Only once during the Council did he yield suddenly to the spirit of mischief which too often guided him; and even then, although Osmyn did not forgive him, it must be owned that the occasion offered fair excuse. For the Rema had insolently assumed that he was ignorant of their laws, in particular of one, which they recommended him to study; and the Kroni and Karngria, not to be behindhand, referred to similiar edicts of their own. Scrolls, parchments were produced, whilst Alvo waited quietly, with eyes cast down as if he knew himself reproved—and then, when the edicts were passed up to him, let them fall from his hand with utmost indifference. Up rose the whole Council in hot indignation. But—

'Sit down,' said Alvo, still more quietly, 'and listen.'

And whilst the Council stood shivering with rage he repeated each law in its own language without a pause. When he had finished there was an instant's silence.

'Is there anything else,' murmured Alvo, 'that you would like to teach your leader?'

'Maravel,' cried the old leader of the Rema in a frenzy, 'to know is not to act.'

'Sit down then, and we will talk.'

They did talk, but the conference was not satisfactory, and the old leader relapsed into a sullen silence. He would never have spoken again if, when the discussion on the laws was over, Alvo had not turned all thoughts to the new tents that were being made. The old leader had his own ideas on tents; he had held them for years, and no one had attended to them. And now, was it possible to refuse a Maravel who asked for advice with such entreating eyes? He despised himself for yielding to the young leader's spell, but it was only for the moment, he would conspire against him to-morrow.

So the Council wore to an end. With a shamed, a burning face, Alvo once more delayed all the payments that were due; and even the Rema forbore to make his position harder, knowing well that Maravel Ursan had not kept his promises. The last formalities followed; and at the conclusion of the meeting, Alvo accompanied his leaders himself to the entrance of his tent. They lingered for a while, feeling the cold air of the night, and looking at the stars above, and the lights of the camp below.

'It is past midnight,' said Alvo. 'Let us sleep.'

He looked so wan that even the commander of the Rema answered,—

'You are tired, Maravel.'

' I have a trick of being tired.'

' That is because you are young.'

But Alvo only smiled demurely.

' If it were not for the traditions of the Alvoi, my face would not be smooth.'

Then they saluted him, and he returned their salute with the slight bend of head and knee with which a young man greets his elders. Leaving him, they went down into the camp, beneath the stars.

' After all,' murmured the chief of the Karngria, ' he treats us with respect.'

' The young leader will not perish for want of fair words,' growled the commander of the Rema. ' But he goes on his own way, notwithstanding.'

Alvo was left with Osmyn—the duties of the day at length accomplished, and preparation for rest the only task. He would not rest, however, till he had restored his tent to order, and he moved about it with quiet hands and steps ; whilst Osmyn, forbidden to assist him, seated himself upon the mattress, and began to repair his own sword-belt carefully. The grim Osmyn had not his master's daintiness, but he attempted to suit his master's taste—no mean attempt if it indeed be true that ' it requires great love to present small offerings.' And now Alvo, having arranged all things to his mind, came to sit down by him upon the mattress.

Alvo was in an unusual mood. Although another man was present, he made no effort to charm or to be playful. He bent his head over the shield he was polishing as if some burden were overwhelming him. The Exiles' Song fell from him, almost in a murmur :—

> Darkly frown the storm-clouds o'er us,
>   Near are sorrow, want, and pain ;
> What care we what lies before us ?

'Osmyn, what didst thou think of my Council ? Praise me.'

He made an effort to shake off his moodiness.

'Estri,' replied Osmyn, who never praised his master, 'what was the use of trying to please them all ? '

'Because that pleases me—Osmyn !'

He threw up both his arms.

'What ails thee, Estri ?'

'I want Ivlon.'

The words sounded like a cry. Osmyn looked at him with undisguised concern.

'He will soon return,' he said, in a grim tone of consolation.

Osmyn did not love the young shield-bearer, but he had no jealousy.

'I cannot endure the camp without him,' Alvo moaned ; 'the hatred, the struggle which never ceases day or night. Osmyn, when we have won

the Fair Country, you shall live with Ivlon and
me, and shall teach us both!'

'That will be impossible, Estri.'

'Because I am so complete a fool?'

'Thou art worse than a fool, because thou couldst
be wise.'

'I tell thee I *cannot* be wise. When we have
won the Alidrah— Osmyn, let us say together the
Prayer to the Great Spirit.'

They repeated it, standing. Then Alvo was
silent for a while. When he next spoke it was in
an altered tone.

'Osmyn, the Gods have some care for us, have
they not? When they know that a man has a
wish, it does not please them to destroy it?'

'Thou hadst better sleep, Estri,' said Osmyn,
and vouchsafed no other answer.

As he rose, Alvo stooped suddenly and kissed
his hand. Osmyn pulled it away in disgust, and
performed his stiff salute, hearing his master's
merry laugh as he went out. He went out into
the cold night and the starlight, and began to pace
up and down outside the tent.

What country does Osmyn seek as he still walks
up and down, weary, disheartened, angry with his
master and himself, calling himself bitterly 'a fool
tied to a fool,' yet giving up his night's rest for his
master's sake? Not the Fair Country, or any
other country, unless there be some land where

devotion is rewarded. Alvo, meanwhile, over-burdened by fatigue, does not know that his follower is losing rest for him.

If in moments when fatigue is almost uncon-sciousness it is possible to be influenced by the thoughts of others, the young leader is in some danger of being dragged in different ways. For, far away by the banks of the Tordrade, Ursan sits alone in his tent, his hard face absorbed in a weary perplexity ; and Ivlon in his dungeon is breathing prayers for his master ; and Olbri raises grateful eyes to the starlit sky. To Alvo, however, over-whelmed by weariness, come no thoughts of Ursan, of Ivlon, or of Olbri. He throws himself on his hard couch, considering ruefully how short a time is left for rest before the dawn. As his head falls, his eyelids close at once with the relief with which a tired child sinks to sleep.

So let him rest—so let us also pause, with one last glance towards those we have learned to know. What shall we say of them—the imprisoned Estri, longing to regain his lost bride and his home ; the wife-maiden, with her lonely, frightened dreams ; the son of the sorcerer, beginning life again ; the old leader, with his weary, plotting head ; the young leader, with his wild fancies, wayward genius. No triumphant chorus, no sure promise of success, would provide fit sentences for any one

of these ; let us rather turn to the familiar, haunting words, which in such little space convey so
much aspiration,—

They seek a country.

END OF VOL. I.

COLSTON AND COMPANY, PRINTERS, EDINBURGH.

www.ingramcontent.com/pod-product-compliance
Lightning Source LLC
Chambersburg PA
CBHW030632030726
47497CB00006B/1743